The Urgency of Now

Dennis Shields

Printed in the United States of America

ISBN: 978-1-935254-74-4

Cover Art by gnibel.com
Book Design by Nadene Carter

First printing, 2012

Dedication

This book is dedicated to my father, Larry Shields, who was a good enough boxer to be the middle weight champion of Princeton University, and to the three greatest American writers of the Twentieth Century, Ernest Hemingway, Eugene O'Neill, and F. Scott Fitzgerald.

While many of their themes remain relevant today, expatriots—drinking too much, living on very little money, and doing very little—are from a by-gone era. I admire O'Neill, Fitzgerald, and Hemingway immensely. I believe they are part of the lost generation—lost and gone, but never forgotten.

This book pays homage to them, their thoughts, their writing styles, and their accomplishments.

"The world, as a rule, does not live on beaches and in country clubs."

—*Letter*, F. Scott Fitzgerald

"We value the worthless and think it holy."

—*God Went Fishing*

"The past is the present, isn't it? It's the future too."

—*Long Day's Journey Into Night,* Eugene O'Neill

Chapter One

Stoli with no vermouth, some ice, and a twist of lime, at four o'clock in the afternoon was the perfect martini at the perfect time, particularly when you drank it with friends in a little café in Paris. The restaurant's interior was dark, with wooden floors, and had that idiosyncratic smell of coffee and pastries and cheap wine. The small windows in front didn't let in much light. The owner had hung some paintings on the walls that weren't half-bad. They, like just about everything in the place, were for sale.

Outside, a light rain swept over the streets. People ducked in for a quick drink and left. The smell of wet wool added an unpleasant element, but not enough to stop us from talking or drinking. I joined a group of reporters who sat at a large, roughhewn table, speaking English, except for Dieter, who mumbled in German. He was from New Jersey and thought it would be better for him if people couldn't understand what he said. Having spoken to him on a few occasions, I thought it showed great perspicacity on his part.

For a moment the sun shone through the clouds, producing a pleasant mist. The owner opened the door. One of the waiters swept the steps and cleaned off the chairs in the hope of drawing more of a crowd.

A red Ferrari approached, radio blasting. The driver stopped, checking to see if the place met his standards or perhaps he was looking for someone. The loud, catchy music had a rhythm that swept through the café. The owner's daughter, who doubled as a waitress when it got busy, was smiling to herself as her body swayed to the music.

The vehicle drove off, and the music with it. The daughter stopped smiling and swaying. She began putting spoons and napkins on all the tables and came over. She asked if we wanted anything else to drink.

We did and ordered another round. Everyone was happy. We drank a lot, laughed a lot, and talked a lot, smoke rising from a dilapidated house, going no place and meaning nothing.

Abandoning his German, Dieter turned to the others at the table and said, "Photographing sports events up close is one thing. Taking pictures of models as they work is a whole other ball game."

"It's the cross I bear," I said.

Dieter was referring to a photo-series I was doing for *Vanity Fair*, called 'The Reality behind the Image,' showing what models were really like. Tonight I was photographing a *European Vogue* photo-shoot.

"They pay you for this, Señor?" Inez, a pretty Spanish reporter, joked.

"More than you would believe," I said.

They laughed and talked of other things. One by one, my friends left until I was the only one at the table. I asked for soup, bread, and the house special. The proprietor was apologetic as he moved me from the big table to a smaller one in a corner. Diners were coming in; he needed the space.

"I understand. Don't worry about it," I said.

Soon, I had a carafe of the house red, which was good. The waiter indicated it was a gift from the owner. Within minutes, fresh bread was on the table and a tasty beef stew, light and flavorful.

I had an assignment at the Pere-Lachaise cemetery that evening. European *Vogue* was doing a "models by generation" piece in the cemetery. Well-known models that had enjoyed success many years before were being photographed alongside young girls on their way up.

I loved the cemetery, with its hills and paths, elaborate statues and ornate tombs placed esthetically in the manicured gardens. I've sat by Jim Morrison's grave for hours. Moliere, Chopin, Proust, Oscar Wilde, and many other talented and famous people were buried there.

Tom Jenkens, a photographer slated to do the work, was an old timer whom the older ladies trusted. Older women had more at stake. They didn't have the luxury of a bad day. Young girls can be photographed in all lights and poses and all kinds of clothes and look fantastic no matter what. Youth has its own geography.

I wondered if *Vogue* was being particularly nasty—a 'where are they now piece' in one of the most famous cemeteries in the world! Could be payback for the arrogance of models in their prime. After all, there is nothing better than arrogance humbled.

After dinner, I walked over to the cemetery. Rolling hills, hundreds if not thousands of trees, winding paths, complex gardens, and the best sepulchres and tombs money can buy, prove that if you can't take it with you, you can at least use it to get a comfortable resting place. Because of the trees and the distance from city lights, all was in inky darkness, silent as the unseen graves.

Six older models were in a state of undress. None wore bras. Breasts disappeared when you were stick thin. Make-up artists tended to the women. PA's were dressing them at the same time, furnishing shoes, hats, and jewelry.

I peered into the darkness, seeing shadowy forms of what I knew were graves. Some of the elaborate statues had lights around their base, distinguishable from the rest of the darkened landscape. I took pictures of the women and the minions working to make them appear beautiful in the hours that lasted before dawn.

The photographer had on loose jeans and an Elvis sweatshirt. He wore a Chicago Cubs baseball cap backwards, with his long gray braid running down his back. He didn't stop talking. He drank. He ate. Snap. Snap. He started taking pictures and, after a while, you listened to him and forgot he was still taking pictures.

The older women were draped in long, filmy ball gowns. The makeup artists had painted their faces a stark white, which hid all flaws, wrinkles, and incipient boniness. Three beautiful young girls, in skimpy bras and panties, tattoos and blocks of color, pink and red eye shadow, and black lip-gloss transforming their faces into inhuman forms practiced acrobatic feats. No soft, bare skin of youth showed up the older ladies.

A male makeup artist, slight of frame, with some acne scars on his face, worked on a woman dressed in gold. Golden makeup glistened over her perfect features. It was Dylan, my Dylan, the most beautiful woman in the world.

Dylan's dress was modest, which surprised me. She had never had plastic surgery and didn't exercise much, but her body was flawless. Her soft breasts, high and yielding, had been photographed often.

Dylan and the make-up person laughed at some shared secret. Dylan got up to get some food and turned away from me. The back of the dress was absent, starting well below her waist, where the bottom of her back and the top of her behind met. Dylan was a perfect woman with a perfect back and a perfect round behind.

Jenkins posed the older models in front of or near the tombs, draped around the stones. The women were beautiful but their whitened faces suggested they were coming out of their final resting places. The choice of the cemetery, then, was not an accident.

The young girls leapt over the grass, doing splits in mid-air, flips, handstands, tumbling madly. They were vital and alive, demigoddesses frolicking in the moonlight.

Golden Dylan glowed among the artifice surrounding her. She was the sole mortal in a group of women returned from the grave. These images, as seen through my lens, were stunning.

Absolute perfection lasts for an instant, but the photographer makes the moment last forever. People would describe me as an excellent photographer, but I knew I wasn't there yet. I was also a writer, but not a good one. I was a nice kid, a capable soldier, and a great drinker. Of all the things to be great at, that's not one most people would pick. For me, it's been very useful.

The sun began to rise as the shoot wound down. Light dew gleamed over the tombstones. The grass was burnished gold, as the rosy hues of the dawn painted skies and rooftops with muted colors. The caterers had set up ornate silver trays filled with various delicacies, sparkling implements, and crystal glasses. The bar was busy, but the food was untouched.

Dylan scavenged among the pristine trays and came back with a hot fudge sundae. The other models were chewing little pieces of celery and spitting them out. Dylan was sucking up the whipped cream and fudge, spooning it sensually in her mouth.

I wanted to hurry to her, but forced myself to move slowly. A man who resembled Aliko Dangote pushed me aside, as Dylan said "Hello darling" to me.

The man stood close to Dylan and asked her, "Do you know who I am?"

"Sure," Dylan said with a smile. "You're the guy who's going to get us some drinks."

The man walked off to do her bidding.

"Can we leave now?" I asked.

"No, I have a few things I have to do, "she told me. "If you want to wait, you can. It won't be long."

"I'll wait as long as it takes," I said, hating myself for saying it as the words came out. I had to be at the La Conte trial at 9:00 AM, and Dylan could take hours deciding what to wear.

I saw an illuminated clock on an unusually tall building in the distance. In this glorious setting, with all its historic and physical beauty, Dylan did the impossible. She stopped time.

I stared at the clock, waiting for it to move. Five minutes turned into an hour, and she was five minutes late anyway.

Then I saw Dylan, in a pair of jeans and a sweatshirt, striding off the set. There should be a special place in Hell for a woman like Dylan but it would be the end of Hell.

A woman I had never seen before stood next to the boy that Dylan had talked to earlier. I was struck with lust. I wanted her so badly. She was beautiful and sexy. She had perfect full lips, voluptuous lips that I wanted for kissing and other things. I wanted her most of all because she wasn't Dylan.

I picked up a glass of red wine, walked over to her, and smiled.

"Hi," I said. "I'm Pete Stanton."

"I know who you are. I love your work."

"Thanks. I'm glad you feel that way because I'm about to embarrass myself. My good friend, Doug Gosling, the greatest living American author, gave me this pick up line. It's the only one I know."

"What is it?"

"He said 'Start by saying my good friend Doug Gosling, the greatest living American author, gave me this pick up line. It's the only one I know. How long does it take for you to know if you'll sleep with someone?'"

"Does that ever work?" she asked, eyebrows rising.

"I'm not sure."

"Twenty seconds," she said. "Let's go."

"So be it," I replied.

We went to her dwelling, which was not very far away. The building was old, with a surly concierge who gave me a nasty look as we walked up the steps. I had my arm around her shoulder and felt her firm young flesh.

She looked up at me with an appraising glance that was a little off-putting. We entered the apartment that I hoped she had rented furnished. The pictures on the walls were posters from Montmartre, faded and tattered. The mustard colored couch did not brighten up the place, and the lamps didn't help either.

It was clean, though, and the glass of wine she gave me was first rate. I sat on the couch and she sat close to me, touching my face lightly with her long fingernails. I shivered and sipped my wine. I was still holding the glass when she began kissing me.

Suddenly a middle-aged woman with a sour expression walked in, muttering in French, followed by a lovely little girl, about five years old or so, wearing a pink nightgown and bathrobe, and furry slippers.

"I knew that was you, mommy. I waited up for you last night," she said, with a charming lisp. She jumped onto the couch, pushed me over, and sat between her mother and me. My companion spoke sharply to the middle-aged woman in bad French, telling her to put the child to bed. She gave her a kiss on the forehead as she lifted her up and tried to give her to the woman.

The little girl started to cry. "I didn't see you all day. You promised to tuck me in me. You promised."

The French woman refused to pick up the child, saying something about her back. Great baby sitter, who couldn't speak English, tending a child who couldn't speak French.

I got up.

"It's okay. Stay with your daughter. It's fine. You really should put her to bed," I said. I noticed a photo of a man standing next to the woman and her daughter, his hand on the young girl's head.

"I should go anyway," I said, as I hurried out the door. It wasn't to be. How could I have thought a second rate Dylan could cure me?

I went home and didn't feel quite right. I felt mildly nauseated. Once you've had cancer, every little thing makes you think it's come back. It's a dark cloud that either puts a governor on everything you do or destroys all inhibitions. Every lump, cough, bruise, nose bleed becomes the beginning of the end, until it's not. It's no way to live. I wished I were brave.

Chapter Two

I slept for a few hours, shaved, showered, and went to the Henré LaConte trial.

The trial was a departure from my usual sports' projects. They needed a photographer in Paris and I was in Paris. The money was good. I can't say it was a compelling story, but I'd done things like this, well sort of like this, in the early days. I could do it now.

Someone discovered that a man named Henré LaConte had been someone else. For sixty-five years, Henré LaConte was Henré LaConte. He got dressed as Henré LaConte, made love to his wife as Henré LaConte, took his children to football matches as Henré LaConte, went to bars, and played darts as Henré LaConte. He was apparently a good-natured fellow who made a decent living, a good husband, father, and grandfather.

For a short time in his life before he was Henré LaConte, he was Pierre Morreaux, a guard at Le Vernet, near the Spanish border. More than forty-thousand refugee Jews were held in concentration camps under French control, and 3,000 died of poor treatment during the winters of 1940 and 1941. The writer Arthur Koestler, who was imprisoned at Le Vernet, said conditions were worse than in the notorious German camp, Dachau.

Pierre Morreaux did his job no worse and no better than anyone else. He was not brutal nor was he kind. He did what, by necessity, he had to do. He was an ordinary prison guard in a death camp.

After sixty-five years, the Simon Wiesenthal Foundation found him. They identified him through DNA, and persuaded the French Prosecutor to try him for his war crimes.

When they first arrested LaConte, they asked him how he felt.

"I'm relieved," he told them. "It is one of the happiest days of my life."

This was not some great political statement. He had lived a lie for many years and was thankful he didn't have to tell it anymore. He seemed a decent sort when I photographed him.

The witnesses all said or remembered nothing. Someone from the Wiesenthal Institute drew the conclusion that Henré was the lynch pin of the entire German war machine. They trotted out inmate 265271, who didn't remember anything. They brought in an old drunken commandant who said Pierre had done a good job, whatever that meant. This wasn't Nuremberg.

At the end of three weeks of nothing, the jury came back with the same verdict—a hung jury. It seemed pointless to retry him. The jury would always have three anti-Semites on it. We were in Paris.

I was sick of France. I had too many old friends and too many new ones. It was time for me to go home, or at least the home that had been mine for the past eight years. To celebrate my last night in Paris, I decided to meet my friend Bernie Siegel for dinner and a few drinks.

When I called him, he suggested a few sets of tennis.

I agreed. I enjoyed playing tennis with him. He was a great athlete.

Siegel could have been the middle weight champion of Princeton, if they had a boxing champion. I doubt it would have mattered to anyone else. It would have mattered to him.

On one particular Saturday morning while sparring, Bernie broke two boy's jaws. He took the first boy to the infirmary, but lurked behind the others when they brought the second boy in. He heard a cute young nurse say, "What animal did this?"

It was too much for him. A pity that he quit. Maybe if he had continued boxing, his life would have been different. Bernie told me his mother was an emotionally labile woman who caused many scenes. She never forgave him for quitting boxing. This seemed quite odd to me.

I headed over to the courts. I joined Siegel and we began hitting. I enjoyed the sweat.

I could never get to ten. When I was fifteen years old I had a tennis pro who worked at the town park, and gave lessons for eight bucks an hour. She told me I should hit ten shots before I tried to hit a winner. Fifteen years later, playing in Paris with Siegel, I still couldn't get to ten. I lost in straight sets and called it quits.

I arranged to meet Siegel for dinner.

I walked home. I started thinking that most of the trouble in my life came from not being able to get to ten. It's good to think about things, but not to think about them too much.

I showered, shaved, and got dressed. Once again, time had gotten away from me. I hurried to the restaurant so I wouldn't be late.

I was hoping Bernie wouldn't bring his girlfriend with him. I didn't have a high opinion of her.

Siegel would have had trouble with women no matter where he was. He married the first pretty girl who slept with him. She wasn't Jewish and she wasn't nice. She ran off a few months into the marriage. His relationships with women did not improve after the divorce.

The current woman in Bernie's life was manipulative and convinced him that he loved her. She called herself Fiona. She was born and bred in Gary, Indiana and christened Tiffany Jane. Fiona's once willowy form had turned into a stick figure with surgically enhanced breasts. She had become desperate as her looks departed.

Fiona had the singular virtue of having received a substantial divorce settlement. Her favorite expression, which she used often, was that it was much more pleasant to marry for money than to make it on your own.

Siegel was happy enough. The point is a lover's deception destroys the innocent and leaves the guilty with an eternal damnation of self. I'm not sure that Bernie was completely innocent, but Fiona, well, she was completely guilty.

Bernie found things to pass the time somewhat frivolously. He was writing his third novel. He showed it to me. The little I read of it was a lot like him, flawed but with some personality and a surface attractiveness.

I walked into a hole-in-the-wall restaurant that Fiona had suggested. I was surprised because it wasn't Fiona's kind of place. Large antique oak mirrors on the wall, with matching benches underneath, reflected the expanse of empty tables and chairs. The place was deserted.

A waiter got up from a table where he was reading *Le Monde* and escorted me to a table near the kitchen. Since there were ten other vacant tables nearby, I raised my eyebrow. He nodded, then seated me at a table near a window.

I sat down on the hard, uncomfortable oak bench.

"Will you be dining alone?" the waiter asked.

"No," I said. "My friends will be here soon."

He looked at me as though he didn't believe me.

I asked for a beer. He nodded, doing nothing. After a moment he handed me the beer menu.

"I'll have a Kronenbourg 1664," I said.

The waiter sneered. He came back about ten minutes later with my drink and the menu. There were few items, peasant food, again, not Fiona's kind of place. I looked at the prices and understood. I laughed. Fiona believed that overpaying was a sign of class.

It was, just not the class she aspired to.

I drank my beer and then another.

Siegel and Fiona walked in and sat down with me.

"Bernie's heading back to the states, *sans* Fiona," she told me.

"I know, we're flying back together," I said.

"I thought you didn't know when you were leaving, Bernie," Fiona said.

"Absence makes the heart grow fonder," I offered.

"You can come with me or not. I don't care," Siegel said. We sat at the table for what seemed to be an eternity, with no one speaking.

The waiter returned and said "The kitchen is backed up. Food will be ready in twenty minutes."

I looked around the room and saw no one.

"I feel like a condemned man waiting for his last meal being told, 'Sorry, there are budget cuts...'" I said.

Siegel laughed. Fiona didn't. Finally, the waiter brought some bread, a saucer of olive oil, and three large steins of cold beer.

I began drinking, concentrating on the icy beverage. Fiona savagely broke off a piece of bread and shoved it in the oil, splashing the viscous liquid everywhere.

Surprising us all, a waiter rushed to the table and wiped it off, replacing the saucer and pouring more oil into it.

"I've just about finished my novel. I'm not sure it's very good," Siegel said.

"I read it. It's extraordinarily mediocre," Fiona offered.

"Thanks," Siegel said.

"Not surprising—to be a good writer you have to experience things. You can't replace living with research," Fiona muttered.

"My, my, aren't we all the literary critics. Have you ever written anything?" I asked her.

"I would have written a masterpiece, but I couldn't find a pen," Fiona replied.

"I've got to look for new representation. My agency went under." Siegel said, and drank some water. He turned to look at a pretty woman walking by.

Fiona glared, her botoxed forehead smooth, her neck almost wrinkle free, her eyes hard.

"What are you looking at?" she asked.

Bernie didn't say anything.

"I'm leaving if you're going to pay attention to every other woman in the place."

Fiona left.

Siegel said, "I can't even look at a woman. Fiona abhors it."

Poor sap, I thought. I found him entertaining, but he was dancing to a pretty ugly tune.

Chapter 3

I was up three hours later. I went to get pastry and coffee. It was a beautiful morning. I enjoyed my *café au lait*, read the papers, and smoked a cigarette. I felt good.

Students hurried to their classes. Employees hastened to their jobs. Sanitation workers swept away the detritus of the evening. Women hosed the front steps of maisonettes. I stepped back in time to another world, another life.

I walked back to the hotel savoring the moment, passing a little gift shop called *Une Boutique de Cadeaux*. It would be a good place to get something for my mother. She loved getting trinkets from the cities I visited. I walked down a few steps and went inside.

I saw items from all over the world: The Eiffel Tower, the Leaning Tower of Pisa, and the Statue of Liberty. There was a small globe on a stand, which you could turn upside down and see a snow scene at the Chateau Frontenac in Montreal. Next to it was a globe with the World Trade Center. It was so old that when you shook it, it didn't look like snow. It looked like ashes. It was horrible. I walked out quickly.

After September 11th and my brother's death, I joined the Army to make the world safe for democracy. If it hadn't been for that day, I wouldn't be here. I don't know where I'd be, but it wouldn't be here. I guess I should be happy to be anywhere. I was living on borrowed time.

Once I was diagnosed, I didn't know whether to occupy my time living or dying. I suppose I chose living. I never talked about my disease because I didn't want pity or compassion. I just kept going, trudging the long and weary road.

It worked better that way.

I got to the airport early, and went to the American Airlines first class lounge. Siegel wasn't there yet. I drank a few Bloody Marys while I waited, laughing to myself as I realized my punctuality afforded me the opportunity of having a few drinks in peace and quiet.

I loved this place. The lounge was all glass and chrome, with grey leather seats, plus grey carpeting, and a long steel and chrome bar. A wide mirror behind the bar reflected light from the windows. Plants softened the hospital-like setting. A pretty girl behind the bar smiled sweetly. It was an idyllic sojourn in the midst of chaos.

I went into the bathroom and prepared my little kit of pills. I religiously performed the ablutions of a peripatetic photographer, rituals done meticulously, in dangerous, dusty airports in third world countries, and in luxurious settings such as these.

I checked: cameras charged, sunscreen, hat at the ready, dysentery pills—and others, extra socks and a pair of shoes, spare set of clothing, any instructions of any kind, memorized and discarded, and above all—a small bottle of vodka.

When I came back to the lounge, I looked around and didn't see Fiona. Siegel had a jacket and tie on, looking polished and hopeful. He was sitting at the bar, reading a book. He looked up at me and smiled.

"Free at last," Bernie said. "Fitzgerald got it right. 'All life is just a progression toward, and then a recession from, one phrase—I love you.'"

"That's not how I see love," I said.

Bernie sat, drinking orange juice. "It's not just about love. I've been doing a lot of thinking, Petey. My life is wrong, all wrong. I've stopped trying to understand why. It does me no good. The point is how can I change it."

"Good point," I agreed.

I knew a little bit about Siegel's unusual childhood. He had been scarred. Bernie's relationship with Fiona was not something any normal man would have chosen.

"I have to be careful and keep in control. I've always been afraid of what I would do if I let myself go," he said.

I wasn't sure where this was going.

"I'm emotionally stunted," he said.

"Aren't we all," I murmured.

"Not too sympathetic, are you?" Siegel said. "Life has been easy for you—growing up in the farmlands of America, a scholarship to Iowa, and instant fame as a photographer."

"Sure," I said, "baseball and apple pie, loving parents, and the State Fair."

A quick set of images came to mind. My mother crying with joy, my father proudly smiling as my brother got on the school bus with his little lunch box for his first day of school, Thanksgiving Dinner with the family watching football. Me, just happy to be part of a good family—not rich, not poor, but safe.

Another set of images flashed through my brain: my brother's casket wrapped in an American flag, my mother and father sobbing; the immense pain from the bone marrow transplant.

Everybody's life looks better from the outside, and Bernie? He was the ultimate outsider.

"Petey. Petey. What are you thinking about?"

"Nothing much," I said.

"I've got to get out of this rut. I want to do something different," Bernie said.

"Something different for me would be a week in Omaha with a nice woman and home cooked meals," I said.

"I have no interest in that. I want to let loose, be free, run with the bulls, not be bound by the rules of ordinary men."

"Are we talking young boys here? Lots of drugs?"

Siegel looked shocked. "I'm not a pervert."

I laughed at him.

"No, seriously, Peter, I don't want to spend my old age regretting what I haven't done."

I felt sorry for him.

"I don't worry about stuff like that," I told him.

"I want to see the world, experience things."

"It's all the same, Bernie. You bring you with you."

"That's right. I want to get away from me. No family baggage, no regrets, just be free. Find my great love."

"Great loves only exist in fairy tales," I told him.

"I don't believe in fairy tales," Bernie said.

"Your entire life has been a fairy tale," I said.

"Fairy tale life? My grandmother lost her family and her soul in the ovens of Bergen Belsen. She survived by turning in families that harbored Jews. She killed herself in front of my mother, who was only seven. I don't think my mother felt anything after that, not a great quality for a mother."

"I had no idea," I said.

"Who cares? She did what she had to do to survive," he said, answering a question I hadn't asked.

"I want to start living my life."

I felt like I was talking to a wall.

We got on the plane. I started going over the pictures I'd taken. I liked them. Bernie fell asleep. He'd had a hard night. I didn't want to wake him, but I had to go to the bathroom. I put my hand on his shoulder.

"Siegel," I said, and shook him.

He looked up, smiled, and blinked. "Sorry. I didn't sleep much last night."

"Let's switch seats so I don't wake you when I come back."

I headed to the front of the plane. A woman gave me a furtive glance as I passed her. I went into the bathroom. After I finished, I reached into my pocket and fortuitously discovered a few Xanax. I took them and went back to my seat.

I started to doze off. My thoughts turned to Dylan. I remembered when I met her. The Yankees had won the World Series. The universe was once again rational.

I was taking pictures inside the locker room. A beautiful woman was interviewing Joe Torre in the midst of the chaos.

She was wearing a bright red dress. Derek Jeter high fived her ever so naturally as he hurried to his locker. I had never met her, but I felt I'd known her all my life.

I waited for the interview to end. I walked up to her. I couldn't help myself.

"Have we met before?" I asked. "You look so familiar to me."

She looked at me and laughed a sweet laugh. "No, I don't think I've had the pleasure," she said.

"I'm Pete. I'm a photographer for ESPN," I said.

"Hello, Pete from ESPN. I'm Dylan."

Roger Clemens grabbed her and gave her a mighty hug, then whisked her away.

"Do you know who that is?" I asked Steve Mittle, a reporter, trying to figure out how I knew her.

"She's only been on ten thousand magazine covers," he replied.

I could feel my face turning red. What an idiot, I thought.

We made eye contact as she was leaving. She mouthed good bye to me. Two weeks later, when my phone rang, it was her. I was shocked.

"Hi, it's Dylan. I don't know if you remember me. We met at Yankee Stadium. Do you want to meet for lunch or something?"

Remember her? I had thought of nothing else, and I've thought of little else ever since.

I awoke when a fat flight attendant reached up to the overhead compartment to get a blanket for someone, pendulous breasts brushing my face. Glamour had long since departed flying. It was better when the women were stewardesses and couldn't be married and had to be under a certain weight and age. It was better when people got dressed up to fly. It was better before the advent of upgrades, when the people in First Class were classy.

Things looked better before. Things always looked better before. I wondered if I felt that way before I got sick. I didn't get on a plane until I was nineteen. It didn't matter. The point was that I was on a plane at this very moment. This was the time to enjoy life, not to worry about tomorrow or think about yesterday.

Chapter 4

I left Paris because it was time to leave. The city defeated me with its perfection. New York was different. Raw energy pulsed on every street. New buildings were erected in the blink of an eye. People danced to the rhythm of pile drivers and heard the lyrics of new money, new opportunities, new fame. Paris was yesterday. New York is tomorrow.

All things could happen here, and if they didn't, you'd never notice. I worked and drank, met with friends and drank, and took pictures and drank. I could sit outside a little sidewalk eatery on Fifth Avenue, near the Plaza Hotel, and never see a single person I knew.

On a crazy spring-like day in February, I sat at a table drinking in the movement of many people busily going about their day, electricity in the air, the incessant sounds of traffic and sirens and helicopters merging into a booming, buzzing melody.

Couples of all varieties of sex, color, and size walked by, hand in hand. Some women, their eyes moving quickly looking for something better, strolled along, some in pairs, some alone. I found them all profoundly sad. I knew their sadness.

I stayed for hours as the sky darkened, neon signs appeared magically, traffic lights glimmered, and all seemed possible.

I watched one young woman, tall and slender, sporting tight, cheap clothing no woman who wasn't financially rewarded for her favors would wear. She was focusing on me, alone, with about five coffees in front of me. She stood a few feet away, squinting her eyes as though she were trying to figure something out.

The waiter gave her a disparaging glance.

"You don't recognize me, do you?" she asked, in a faint Latino accent that revealed all that she was trying to hide

"I don't think I've had the pleasure, ma'am."

"You took a picture of me that was on the cover of *Time Magazine*."

"Please don't take this the wrong way, but I think I would remember photographing a prostitute for the cover of *Time*."

"I'm not a hooker. I look good. I'm supposed to meet my crew at *Annex*. It's the hottest club in New York."

Annex was strictly bridge and tunnel, but after calling her a hooker I thought better of pointing that out.

"I can't believe you don't remember me. I was tending an ALS patient, drawing blood and joking with him. I told him to watch his hands. You could see death in his eyes, but he was laughing. Somehow your picture exposed pain and joy at the same time. It was a story about hospice care. I'm a nurse."

"That was you?"

A waiter came up to our table. I thought he was going to ask her to leave.

"Please make sure nobody bothers my friend. She was on the cover of *Time Magazine*."

I did not penetrate the waiter's skepticism, but he did not ask her to leave.

"Sweetie, what do you want to drink?" I asked quickly, remembering her but unable to retrieve her name.

"Patrón," she answered, her choice of drinks, if not her style of dress, was upscale and trendy.

"Oh my," I said.

"Oh my," she mimicked. "Waiter, Patrón."

I shrugged, and asked for one as well.

She smiled at me and patted my hand. "So good to see you here," she said, trying to fit in.

The waiter maintained his inscrutable visage. He refrained from expressing his opinion of the woman, if he even had one, and went to get the drinks.

She said, "I'm Liza."

"Pete," I said."

"I know. You have no reason to remember my name, but I haven't forgotten yours. Hello, Pete."

I was beginning to remember her. She had a certain toughness that only New Yorkers have. Looking at her, I recalled how kind she had been. She was a very pretty twenty-four or twenty-five year old. Her makeup diminished her.

"How are you?" I asked.

"I would complain, but who would listen?"

"Don't you like Manhattan?"

She shrugged. "I guess everybody has to be somewhere."

Her accent was heavy, her philosophy shallow.

We drank our Patrón, which picked us up and let us down, none too smoothly. The girl stared into the glass, as though looking for it to refill itself. I knew that look. I knew what she felt. I had experienced it often.

I lifted my empty glass to the waiter. He brought us two more. I decided to take her to dinner. I felt that I owed her something. I won a Deutsche Börse Award for photography and all she got was a picture on *Time Magazine*.

"Can I buy you dinner?" I asked. "Your picture won me an award."

"I'd be honored."

I paid for the drinks.

"You want to go to your apartment or something first?" she asked.

"Nope," I said.

"Why? I'm not good enough," she said, suddenly becoming hostile.

"It's complicated. Let's get something to eat."

We walked for a long while. I stopped at *Nello's,* one of my favorite haunts. I figured I owed her for mistaking her for a hooker. I'd take her for a special meal.

"Is this where we're going?" she asked.

"Trust me, it's very good," I said.

We went into the dining room and sat at a table. She was quite uplifted when the waiter brought her bread, as though she hadn't eaten for some time.

Despite her tough attitude and her garish attire, everything she said reflected kindness and compassion. No matter how she looked, no matter how thick she piled on the make-up, her character shone through. She was a class act in all the ways that mattered. I wanted to get rid of her anyway. It made me feel like a jerk, showing me, one more time, how screwed up my values had become.

Liza finished the loaf and all the butter, without allowing me even a crumb.

"More bread," she growled at the waiter.

A waiter brought over a plate of zucchini with garlic.

"You're okay, you know, maybe a little bit nasty. Why don't you want me?"

"I'm in a relationship," I explained.

"Sure you are."

The waiter brought our main course. She had filet mignon. I had one of the best veal piccattas in the City, the perfect marriage of veal, wine, lemon and butter. Liza kept sampling my dinner without asking me. After the fifth time, I looked at her, annoyed.

"Food always tastes better from someone else's plate," she explained.

I wanted to say something, but decided against it.

I was happy to see my friends, Siegel, Fiona, Mr. and Mrs. Smith, with some people I didn't know, as they were leaving the restaurant. They saw me and hurried over to my table.

Fiona had followed Siegel, despite his instructions to the contrary. She looked Liza up and down, disapprovingly. She bent over and whispered into my ear, "Can't you afford a better prostitute?"

I wanted to stick up for Liza, but had long since given up appealing to the better natures of people who had none. I remained silent.

I got up to greet the rest of them.

"We're debating where we should go. Come along," Smith said.

"You don't know where you're going, but I should go with you?"

"Come on, Petey, we'll go bowling. It's fun." Mrs. Smith said, smiling. "Bowling is the next new rage."

"Do come," Fiona said, with a practiced smile of no great warmth. "And bring your girlfriend."

"Certainly," I said and sat down.

"We'll wait at the bar until you've finished your meal," Smith said. He tipped an imaginary hat as they walked away.

We ate quickly, Liza relishing every bite.

"Come with us," I said.

She looked up at me and smiled.

My God, she's damned good looking, I thought.

We went up to the bar, where they were downing after-dinner drinks, mostly Sambuca and Cognac.

"It's my pleasure to introduce you to the great Liza," I told them. Liza grinned. "She made the cover of *Time Magazine* for her work in a hospice."

They talked to each other, Mrs. Smith being friendly, maybe, and Fiona getting ready to attack. Fiona always attacked. She was very consistent. Normally, consistency is a good quality but not in her case. Why was I not surprised Fiona was in New York?

Liza wasn't cowed by the group, who were more than a little drunk and who talked about going bowling, as if they ever would. I began to admire her more as she proceeded with an amused contempt, treating the others like ill-behaved children who bored her.

A non-descript, well-dressed man, a little long in the tooth, who sometimes came by was holding forth. At first glance he was ridiculous. He was using phrases like "what a great chick" and "hot damn" and "hot stuff". He was immensely wealthy, though, so it worked. Everyone thought he was clever. A billion dollars changes many things, including our opinion of people.

He invited us to his latest venture, *RFD*, a New York Club doing country line dancing, an absurd concept but successful, at least for now. The doorman stopped Liza, but when he saw she was with our group, welcomed her in.

It had been a comedy club for a while, and before that an experimental theatre and earlier, I think, an art gallery. Huge pitchers of beer sat on every table, included in the cover charge, but you could order cognac and wine. People filled the dance floor. It was a mob scene.

The band was French, and the men sang with what they thought were American accents, lending a surreal tone to an already bizarre event. The proprietor played an old fiddle well, joining the band for a few numbers. Everyone danced with enthusiasm. I think the owners of the club kept the heat on high, so people would order more drinks.

"I'm sweating like a pig," Liza said.

"Do you have a card?" Smith asked.

I was pretty sure he thought she was a prostitute. It was an honest mistake.

"I don't think so," she said. "I'll give you my number."

She found a pen and wrote her number on his hand.

At that point I left Smith and Liza by the dance floor and went to the bar. It was very warm. I ordered a coke, probably the most authentic thing in the place. The incredible violinist sounded like he was from the foothills of Appalachia. I walked to the doorway of the club and stood there, feeling the coolness of the wind. A few taxis pulled up and a limo.

A pack of Wall Street assholes in their Valentino suits, Zegna shirts, and Prada shoes, one or two with sunglasses on, walked down the street, speaking excitedly. Their hair was perfectly coifed, their faces deeply tanned, their gestures dramatic, overdone and theatrical. Dylan was with them. She was beautiful, as always, and seemed to be very much a part of the crowd, which streamed rapidly into the club.

Eyeing Liza, one of them said, "Look what we have here, a working girl. How charming. I think I will dance with her."

A few of his friends cheered him on.

One of them shook his head. "Shame on you, boy. Shame on you."

The rest laughed as though they owned the world. Dylan laughed out loud, enjoying their effrontery. Their over-the-top arrogance infuriated me. I hated them for picking on someone who was making the best of the little she had. Who were they, after all?

I walked away from them in disgust. I figured I'd get myself a drink and went to the bar. I ordered a whiskey with a beer chaser.

A very thin beautiful young woman sat at the bar, talking to a friend.

Her friend asked, "How do you stay so skinny? What's your diet?"

"Heroin," she responded calmly.

"Oh," said the friend excitedly. "That's great, but aren't you afraid you'll get addicted?"

"No, I don't even like it."

Oh yes, I thought.

I finished my drink. Time to return to my own crowd. I came back to see Liza dancing with one of the boys, and then another. They would all dance with her and think they had done something grand or clever.

I sat at a table with Siegel. Fiona was dancing with someone I vaguely knew, far too young for her. She danced well. Mrs. Smith introduced me to a man named Eliot Goldstein, explaining he had been morbidly obese and a failed inventor, until he invented the automatic laser flush toilet. He lost weight and became a man of leisure.

I must say I wondered what he was doing here and what I was doing with him. I can't say his conversation sparkled. It might have, if he had said anything.

I was leaving the table when Eliot said "I saw your war pictures at MOMA. To be perfectly frank, I didn't get what the big fuss was about."

I should be dancing with Liza, I thought. I got up and walked toward the dance floor. She was looking better and better.

"Don't let him bother you. He's young—and he's from New Jersey," Mrs. Smith said, coming up behind me.

"Young is one thing, but young and stupid is another."

"Oh pay him no mind. He's just come out of a bad divorce, his second. She was a younger version of his first wife, with less charm, which one would have thought impossible. She slept with any man or woman who showed her the slightest interest, except Eliot."

What could you say to that?

Mrs. Smith didn't stop. "She spoke badly of everyone. I believe there's nothing worse than talking behind someone's back. The best thing you could say about the second ex-Mrs. Goldstein is that after she left, she was gone. By the way, your friend seems to be having a great success."

"Of a different kind. At least she knows the score."

Mrs. Smith smiled her warm smile that reached her eyes, but her forehead remained smooth, detracting from the illusory warmth.

Bernie came up to me and said, "Where'd you disappear to?"

"Nowhere."

"Hello honeys." Dylan came over. She was a breath of crisp, cool, perfumed air.

"Of all the gin joints, in all the towns, in the world..." I said. "Not drinking tonight?"

"Very little," she said.

"This is my friend, Bernie Siegel," I said. "Bernie, this is Dylan."

He reached out his and shook Dylan's, holding her hand tightly.

She pulled her hand out of his and looked at me.

Dylan had been discovered at an assembly at the Spence School in Manhattan. She became the Face of Chanel at fifteen. After years of runway modeling, cover shoots, late night drinking, and too many pills, she was still slender and shapely, with a deep bosom that owed nothing to plastic surgery. In the land of the airbrushed plasticized Barbies, even Dylan's laugh lines were magnificent. She made the thin look skinny and the curvaceous fat.

"Where do you find these people?" I said.

"Lovely, aren't they, but what of your friend?"

"Can't hold a candle to you, my dear, but she outshines this crowd."

"You're wrong, Pete. You know this is an insult to all decent women," she laughed.

"So show me some," I said.

"Show you some what?" she asked.

"Decent women," I laughed.

"I want to dance with you now," Dylan said.

We danced.

Siegel stood at the bar Staring at hertransfixed by her beauty.

I shivered and wondered if this would be one more Dylan conquest, if she would even bother.

We danced. It was hot and crowded, but I felt happy. We passed Liza, dancing with yet another of the Masters of the Universe.

"I like your whore," Dylan said.

"If you want, you can have her," I replied.

We got off the dance floor. Fiona came up to us, trying to contain her anger, her face a little ugly.

"Won't you introduce me to your friend?" she asked. "Does she work with Liza?"

Dylan looked at her with a half-smile. She turned to me and said, "You know, Petey, there's nothing sadder in life than when a woman doesn't know when to hang up her thong."

Fiona said nothing.

Dylan took my arm and guided me toward the door.

Siegel waved as we walked by. "Goodnight Bernie," I said.

Dylan ignored him as we headed out.

"You're such a romantic," Dylan said, looking disdainfully at Liza, who was sitting with Dylan's friends. I didn't like Dylan just then, but knew the feeling would go away. Dylan could get away with anything; any woman who looked like Dylan could get away with anything.

We walked a few blocks. It started to rain, a light mist, that New York rain that rendered the city clean and new. I felt almost blissful as I gazed at Dylan.

I saw tears running down her face.

"Petey," she said, "I'm so unhappy."

Chapter 5

We hailed a cab. The taxi was old, a gypsy cab with probably a hundred thousand miles on it. It chugged down the street. Lighted bars and late-closing shops sparkled. Few people walked on the streets and few lights were on in the apartments lining the thoroughfare.

The cab was dark. I smelled her, her hair, her warm body. I tried to kiss her.

"No," she said faintly.

"Why?" I asked her. I understood. I didn't want to understand. I wanted to connect with her, to comfort her, to love her.

"We could..." I started to say.

"No," she said mournfully. "That makes it worse."

The taxi turned into a well-lit street near Penn Station. Her flawless face, with her sparkling blue eyes, came into focus. Her voice sounded as though she were in pain, but her visage was as serene as an antique Japanese woodcut.

"This is difficult for me," she said.

"Don't say that. Everything isn't always about you."

"I know. These are your issues."

"I'm in love with you. That's all that matters."

Dylan sat motionless in the cab, her head down, her body still. I thought how perfect she was, how beautiful her skin, her eyes, her nose, her mouth. She turned and caught me staring at her.

"Pete, I love the way you look at me. It makes me think of Yeats's poem to Anne Gregory—you know the one? 'Only God could love you for yourself alone and not your yellow hair.' You and God, Petey. You and God."

I felt my face turning red. My heart pounded to the rhythm of a wonderful song. She was wrong about me, of course, but I was happy she felt that way.

We'd arrived at the park, driving through the entrance on Central Park South. The famous tourist trap with all the white lights, as though every day were Christmas, was now dark, with one solitary white light shining. One small bird, I thought, a swallow, flitting about. One swallow does not a summer make, nor one kiss a love affair. One moment of perfect bliss sometimes is nothing more than that, but my soul was filled with joy, my heart replete with hope.

My spirit sang, exhilarated. I could make this beautiful, perfect, difficult woman happy. Joy, bliss, and gratitude coalesced in this fabulous moment when all was right with the world. Everything would be wonderful. Everything was wonderful.

"Let's go to Cipriani's," Dylan said. "I'm bored."

In an instant my perfect moment vanished.

The taxicab driver pulled over to the side of the road. He turned around to look at us. Dylan stared into the seat, maintaining a monumental, sulky silence.

"Oh, go to Cipriani's," I told the cabbie. Lights in the distance illuminated nothing.

Dylan moved restlessly. She knew I was annoyed.

"Kiss me," she said.

"No," I said. Anger filled me. I couldn't breathe. I sat there, heart hardened but pounding so forcefully I thought it would burst. Why does she play these games? Why could she not be—just content?

When the cab stopped, I thrust some money at the driver and got out.

Dylan tried to give me her hand as she stepped out of the cab, but I shook it off. We walked into Cipriani's, lush, heavy wood, plush carpets, dark and ornately designed. Our little crowd was sitting at the bar.

"Hello, honey," Dylan drawled at someone, pure sex in her voice. "I want a drink."

"Pete, Dylan," called Mrs. Smith. "You have to meet my friend, Anthony Scarfo. Everyone calls him Dodo." She pronounced his name with the emphasis on the first syllable.

"Hello," Dylan said, her face redrawn into a mask of caring.

"Dodo, this is the fabulous Dylan. Dylan, the fabulous Dodo."

Dodo was a large man whose expensively tailored clothes obscured his girth. He bowed to Dylan as Smith called out, "Petey, do you know Liza carries a knife? When she pulled it out of her garter, the bouncer knocked her out."

Dodo waved the fight away, getting to the more serious business of having the waiter bring Dylan a drink.

Smith tried again. "Good looking girl, though. She's got something. Have a drink."

"No," I told him, "I've got work to do in the morning."

I could hear Mrs. Smith muttering to herself in the background.

"I would make a great widow," she said.

Like the rest of the crowd, I ignored her.

"My husband can be very gracious," she offered, again with that wonderful smile. Mrs. Smith had an uncanny ability to be bitchy without saying a word.

I nodded to Dylan, standing at the bar. Dodo was buying champagne. Dylan took a flute and raised it high, silent until everyone looked at her.

She recited:

> When old age shall this generation waste, Thou
> shalt remain, in midst of other woe.
> Than ours, a friend to man, to whom thou say'st,
> "Beauty is truth, truth beauty," –that is all ye know
> on earth, and all ye need to know.

"That was lovely, my dear," Dodo said. "I shall drink to you."

He tipped his glass toward her and then emptied it. "Now let us have some more."

That would be delightful," Dylan said, as she sipped her champagne.

"Heavenly," I said. "Simply exquisite, but I fear I have to leave. It's late, and I have to be up early tomorrow."

"Really going?" Dylan asked. There was no supplication in her voice. She was indifferent and had no desire to hide it.

Dylan raised her glass. She waited until everyone was quiet.

"Everything is rainbow, rainbow, rainbow! And I let the fish go," Dylan said, trying to repeat her past success.

"Profound but not very original," I said.

She laughed and asked, "Weren't you leaving?"

Dodo maintained his air of cordiality, as though he were playing a part in a play for which he had no particular affection.

I felt relief as I walked out of Cipriani's and down the quiet streets. Delivery trucks were beginning their rounds, making music punctuated by muted words. The moon was still in the sky, painting the city with new life, new promise. I saw it for the lie that it was as I trudged back home.

I wanted to go to sleep but it wasn't going to happen.

My place was small. Dylan's crowd would have scorned it. I didn't care. I lived over a bar. I always wanted to live over a bar. Trucks carrying produce to the markets downtown and to the Bronx clattered and shook, making it hard to sleep. I looked at myself in the large mirror over the dresser, seeing a pathetic, desperate man.

God, did I hate self-pity. Dylan brought out the worst in me. I wanted her so much and there was nothing I could do about it. I felt like I was back in the hospital in Iraq. You know in the old days, you died. War was hell and it was over. Not anymore. The war meant nothing. It just left me with new horrors.

After my injury, I recovered at Walter Reed. On one side of me was an Air Force Captain whose helicopter crashed.

Not too many captains got hurt. Danger was reserved for the rank and file.

On the other side was a skinny black kid from Alabama everybody called the Salamander. He'd lost both legs looking for land mines. I'd been sweating all night which was surprising because my punctured lung and cracked ribs were pretty much healed.

I felt a lump under my arm.

"I got this lump under my arm. Do you think it's anything?" I asked Salamander. "It hurts."

"Boss, it always start with a lump or a bruise or a cough, and ends with a coffin closing," the Salamander told me.

"Ya think?" I said.

"Nah. Just messing with you, man. But I'd wait til I get out of this hospital, and show it to a real doctor."

I followed Salamander's advice, which probably saved my life, at least for the time being.

A year later, I met Dylan. She was a reporter for a television station. She had made two movies, which she couldn't bear to watch, neither one of which was particularly popular. Somehow she didn't film right. The camera didn't love her. Maybe she was all illusion, and the video camera couldn't pick it up.

This was by no means a deterrent to the many directors who wanted her to grace their films. Everything always worked out for Dylan. That's the way it was. It didn't mean anything.

To hell with her. To hell with me. Being told somebody had it worse was no comfort. It made me feel trivial.

I lay in bed, my mind doing calisthenics, thinking of Dylan and her body and what it would be like to be whole and be with her. My body was filled with longing, a longing that could never be satiated. I felt my body floating in the ocean as I waited to be dragged under.

The problem with doing drugs is when you're not doing them it makes life unbearable and slow. After awhile, I got quiet and my eyes got heavy.

I was in a sound sleep.

Dylan called. "Let me up," she said.

I buzzed her in and opened the door.

Dylan came into the apartment, soused.

"Hello, Dylan. This is a surprise."

"Petey, they bore me so. I wanted to see you."

I started making a drink.

"What's Dodo like?" I asked. I thought of Joseph Conrad, referring to one of his characters as being 'one of us,' primarily because he wasn't, and said, "Oh right, he's one of us."

"Aren't we all?" Dylan asked.

"I wish I were," I replied, and poured her some whiskey.

"Please, Petey, it's too late to get started on that," she said, as she took the glass I gave her.

"Oh my," I said. "Just one drink." I guess I wasn't particular either.

Dylan seemed indifferent. It was late. I was tired and wanted to go to sleep.

"You're no fun," she pouted.

"You made that clear last night," I said.

She looked at me and knew I had had enough. Maybe that was her best talent, knowing when to stop. That meant she could always start again.

She kissed me on the top of my head and walked away.

After Dylan left, again, to be with a fat man with a lot of money, the truth came at me like a left-hander's jab. I couldn't avoid it, and I couldn't forget.

Chapter 6

March came in like the proverbial lion, roaring its displeasure with the changes time wrought. Bitter winds and cold rains beat down on the just and the unjust, the blessed and the damned. The eighth was the day; the appointment made the previous year. A nurse had telephoned to remind me, as though I would forget.

My mother called to ask how I felt.

I said fine and yes, I was going, and no, I didn't want her to come with me. It's hard enough to be afraid alone but harder still to have to be brave for others.

Fifth year anniversary and the odds go up that you'll survive. What is an anniversary, a beginning or an end? Probably both.

I walked the twenty-five blocks to New York Hospital, not wanting to hear the news unless it was good news. How to avoid the inevitable? An oxymoron if I ever heard one.

I entered the far too familiar building and rode up in an elevator with a little girl and her father, standing close together, hand in hand. I hoped he was the sick one.

I sat in a hard plastic chair in the spacious waiting room. All the magazines were out-of-date. I thought it was intentional. Old romances of movie stars are like stale bread. Looking about, I could feel the ebb and flow of life, and that it would go on. It would go on, even if I weren't here to see it.

After forty-five minutes, the pleasant woman behind the desk called my name and smiled at me. All the women working there smiled at the patients, as though they remembered them, even if they'd just started working in the office a few weeks before.

They gave you blue paper robes. I never could figure out how to put them on or where to tie the ties, also paper, which ripped in my thick, clumsy hands. Terror worked in battle. It energized you and helped you act like a hero. There were no heroes in blue paper robes, even if you put on two, one back to front, one front to back.

A tech walked me into an examining room. I knew the drill. I didn't like needles. I didn't like bubbly young blonds comforting me and calling me by my first name. They were too familiar. It was rude.

The girl drew and drew and drew more blood. The vein stopped giving. The young phlebotomist went to work on the other arm.

My doctor was a good doctor and a good man, named Turk. He could be curt and surly, but he knew what he was talking about. I didn't need a good bedside manner in a doctor, and he didn't have one.

"Energy?"

"Good."

"Check. Any blood in stool or urine?"

"No."

"Check. Night sweats?"

"All good, doc."

"Great. Great. You still impotent?"

"Yeah."

"Unfortunately that can be a side effect of the chemo."

"That's some side effect, Doc," I said.

"You look good. Strong. You might want to cut down on the booze and pills."

"I might not," I said. I had no bedside manner either.

"I'll call you in a few days with the results. Pee in the cup on your way out."

I complied.

I was nauseated from the whole deal. I used to worry from the moment I walked out the door. I jumped every time the phone rang.

Now, though, I didn't care. I realized, it is what it is. Each day I wanted to live slightly more than I wanted to die.

I walked down the hall and into the media room. I needed to sit down. I saw babies, kids, walking around with IV's attached to them. Some of them smiled and laughed as they waited. Others were somber. All had a look in their eyes that tore me apart. They had seen death up close. No child should see that.

A boy who looked to be about ten challenged me to a game of Guitar Hero.

We played for almost an hour, even though he grew fatigued. He had surgery scheduled the next morning. I had things to do, but I couldn't leave. His grandmother came to take him for pre-op tests. There was a story there, not a pleasant one, and not one I wanted to hear. She hugged me before they left.

I tore off the hospital bracelet and walked the seven floors to the lobby. No more sick people for me.

I stopped for a quick lunch, and a well needed drink at Fresco's, a media haunt. It was late enough so I expected to find no one I knew. Unfortunately, there were people there I knew, even Smith.

"You're looking fresh, Petey," he said. "These late nights are killing me. Bernie's trying to get me to play tennis. I don't even like tennis, and I like playing with him even less. I think he's looking for you."

A woman I knew, an attractive young reporter from *The Chicago Tribune*, came in. I beckoned her over. She had the annoying voice of a clucking chicken. No matter what she said, all I heard was cluck, cluck, cluck.

"Let's go someplace else," I said. "Maybe P.J. Clarks—the best cheeseburgers in the city."

"Cluck, cluck, cluck," she said.

"Where do you want to go?" I asked.

"Cluck." All I heard was cluck.

"Maybe next time."

"Cluck, cluck, cluck."

Shut the cluck up, I thought.

Smith was sitting at a table with another friend, Shri Ghoti, the famous Pakistani eulogist for the *New York Times*.

"Hey, Petey I'd like your opinion on this," Shri said. "He was a most generous man, who shared everything he had. Unfortunately, he was very poor, so mostly he shared nothing. What do you think?"

"I think it's wonderful," I said.

Smith ignored us. Smith was interested in what he was interested in, and everything else was noise.

"How about introducing me to your exquisite friend? I'd like to take her away with me," Smith said.

"What about Mrs. Smith?" I asked.

"Leave fidelity to the poor," he replied.

On that note I headed home. I needed sleep.

The New York air was crisp and clean. I got a text from Siegel, asking me to meet him on 45th and 7th.

I hurried over and saw him standing on the corner.

"You hungry?" he asked.

"No food for me, but I'll have a drink. I only have an hour or so."

"How about that new *tapas* place around the corner?"

I agreed, and we started walking.

An old homeless man had set himself up in the recess of a brownstone next to the restaurant. He was wearing combat pants and a rumpled, red wine-stained shirt from a Grateful Dead concert, but the picture was faded and some hopefully unascertainable substance covered the letters. He held a sign that said 'Please help me. I'm hungry. How about a thousand dollars?'

I laughed. Only in New York, I thought, as we walked in.

In the restaurant, Bernie picked out the tapas he wanted and cerveza for both of us, which came immediately. I looked out the window and saw a tawdry place across the way, the windows dark and dirty, a neon sign flashing. 'Girls! Girls! Girls!' mocking me.

"How have you been?" I asked.

"Just passing the time. How's your girlfriend Liza?"

I looked at him. "She's not my girlfriend."

"I know. She was not a hoot, by the way. I may be old fashioned, but there are limits. Wives and girlfriends should not meet and prostitutes should be left for the bedroom," he said. "My father taught me that."

"She's not a prostitute. She cares for the ill," I told him.

"Call it whatever you want," Siegel said.

"It must be nice to know everything," I said.

"I don't know everything, but I know one thing. I'm tired of Fiona. She only wants to be with her own kind, provided they're older and weigh more. I don't think we'll last much longer but I do feel sorry about it. I guess I have a sense of obligation."

Fiona was content in her rut. Siegel was breaking out. He was calm because he'd never been tested. I had a feeling that was all about to change. People like him, who come late to life, who are put in the game a few minutes before it's over, tend to do much worse than those who've been playing their entire lives.

Bernie was eating dish after dish without noticing what he was eating. He got a text message from Fiona and said, "Sorry, I've got to go meet her." He got up and left.

Fiona did not evoke compassion. No one cried for a woman with no tears for anyone but herself. There had been plenty of unpleasantness for years, and none of it Bernie's.

Pathology always trumps cognition. Bernie could think what he wanted. It still would be very hard for him to break loose.

I knew too much about doing the right thing and how difficult it was. I remembered how things ended with Dylan. She had broken my heart. Maybe Dylan wasn't capable of being faithful, but that was the one flaw I couldn't forgive. We'd been together for about six months when she nonchalantly told me about a sexual encounter with a masseuse earlier that day at the Mondrian Hotel.

"Honey, it was a moment of weakness, but he had such good hands and he was so cute. What could a girl do?"

I told her I loved her and when she was ready to commit just to me, I would be there for her.

She said she would let me know.

I asked every day until I stopped asking.

It took me a long while to get over that and maybe I never have.

I started to see other women. Around that time, my white blood cell count dropped and they changed my medication. After that, for whatever the reason, I was unable to have sex.

I saw numerous specialists. They couldn't figure it out.

Turk made a differential diagnosis: It was the new medication.

I made my own diagnosis: Dylan.

The months went by and I still couldn't perform.

I've almost stopped trying.

Perhaps it's God's way of telling me to wait for Dylan. When you look like Dylan, the world conspires to help you.

Whatever.

Chapter 7

I headed over to The Plaza for a drink and was delighted to see my old friend Rusty Baron sitting in the lobby. I met the attorney when I photographed him for the cover of *Esquire Magazine*. I positioned him sitting in the Jacuzzi on his 200-foot yacht, smoking a big Cuban Cigar. It was meant to be ironic. The yacht, *No Smoking*, which he paid for from his fee in the case against the tobacco industry, replaced his 185-foot yacht, *Mine's Bigger*.

Time portrayed Rusty as David of David and Goliath fame, but he saw himself more as Don Quixote, a hopeless romantic who was always fighting windmills.

"Except my windmills are real," he'd said. "They're the pharmaceutical companies that murdered the little girl in Lubbock, Texas, and the big oil company that blew up eleven people and destroyed the Gulf; the chemical company that poisoned the water and annihilated a town for a few miserable shekels. I stand side by side with the victims, arms flailing, legs kicking, screaming and swearing to get justice."

Rusty Baron was a great orator, quoting Cicero, Aristotle, and Yogi Berra, with equal ease. His voice switched from Shakespearean actor to television preacher to Mississippi shrimp worker. He was short with white hair. He had an incredible appeal. You instantly liked him and found him delightful.

When I saw him at the Plaza, Rusty smiled and, in his endearing southern drawl, said, "In a sea of weeds, how lucky I am to find a daisy."

"What are you doing in New York?" I said.

"I'm here to enforce the last bastion of liberty, the juror system. A jury said the Chinese government should pay for all the havoc they wreaked. They have spoken. I'm here to collect."

He was in town to seize a Chinese freighter that sat in New York Harbor. He loved the fireworks.

"You're always trying to do what's right," I said.

"That's what I do," he said. "How, my friend, are you doing? There's a sadness to you."

"What's the difference? In a couple of hours I'll be drunk, and it won't matter."

"In a couple of hours, I'll be sober, and it won't matter either. I have to leave. I do enjoy a tipsy walk down Fifth Avenue."

"Good luck tomorrow," I said.

"God speed," he replied, tipping his hat as he left.

Baron left me alone with Grama, the bartender. I was never sure if that was his first or last name. Grama was a most sophisticated fellow. His major virtue was his apparent discretion. His major vice—his discretion was for sale.

He had his share of malice, too. He had an advanced Harvard degree in philosophy, awarded a short time before. The job market being what it was, he made more money behind the bar. If things changed, Grama could return to philosophy. If not, he could buy a bar somewhere and philosophize to his heart's content.

He told me he hadn't seen Dylan in days.

I briefly stopped in the lobby, hoping to run into Dylan. I went to another of my favorite cafes, crossing the great divide to Brooklyn. The river looked beautiful, reminding me of the many destinations left to me.

New York was a city with many rivers. Crossing from one side to the other meant journeying to a very different place. Each street was pregnant with possibilities. It was a city that took a long time to get to know, streets laid out in precise fashion notwithstanding. That Siegel couldn't do it was not surprising and might have told me that he wasn't a romantic or a realist. Some fantasists are like that, and want neither dreams nor facts but instead sense data to confirm their wild flights of fancy. They mistake consistency for meaning.

New York wasn't the city for them. This was a city of crime and riots, poets and playwrights, and painters and thinkers, a mélange of thousands of miles and several languages, separated by any two adjacent streets.

I decided to take a little stroll on the Promenade before going to the restaurant. I wanted to see something lovely enough to justify staying in New York, living here and not leaving.

The blur of the smog-covered walkway, the dust and haze hovering above gave a painterly quality to Brooklyn, making it stunning and obscure. Homeless men muttered angrily to themselves, fixtures on these streets. One man was yelling aloud, punching the air with angry fists. A thin woman wearing three ragged sweaters, dirty jeans, her bare feet filthy, pushed a shopping cart filled with bags and torn newspapers. She looked at me and then swiftly away.

And then back to looking at the river and the skyline of Manhattan, bereft of the twin towers, past and future merging into a wonderful present. I sighed and walked onto Montague Street where I grabbed a cab.

The cab left me not far from the River Cafe, maybe my favorite bar in New York.

Martin Saunders sat at a table in the little patio behind the restaurant, popular in summer, less so now, because it was cold. Winter winds verified their existence by sweeping over weather vanes and bits of rope and trees off in the distance. You can only see the wind, you know, by its effects on other objects, by its effects on Marty. He had long since lost the ability to interact with anything other than his thoughts.

The guy was sipping an espresso and staring at the river. He seemed to be a permanent fixture, a silent statue, attesting to the ability to be consumed by self. His thinning hair was disheveled, his light jacket coffee stained, and his face a testament to a long life of betrayal by those he thought were friends.

Funny, though, he was more the betrayer than the betrayed. Marty was always up to something. He was the kind of guy that if there was a long way around the block, he'd find it.

"So you finally showed up," he said. "I've been looking for you for days. You are one busy photographer."

"Everything okay?" I asked him, knowing that he'd be asking for money in a moment or two.

"Sure, right as rain," he said.

"So what's happening?"

"I don't have a clue. I'm finished with it all. I don't even have money to eat."

I doubted that.

"Do you know what I realized, Petey? Do you know what my newest, latest, most informative epiphany is?" he asked.

"What?" I said. He still had some brain cells left but it was a mistake to talk to him.

"My greatest realization is that, knowing what I know now, I would make the same mistakes again. If I rejected one woman, I'd find one who was worse, same with jobs, same with where I'd live. I would make the same mistakes again," Martin Saunders, once a perceptive, successful journalist, said, repeating himself in one paragraph.

Anyone repeated himself if he talked long enough, but there is a certain ability to be able to do it in the same paragraph.

"When I get this way, I want to be alone," he said.

I knew what he wanted. I gave him some money. He was a broken man but I liked him nevertheless. We went back a long way.

"Thanks," he said.

"Let me get you something to eat."

"No, I think I'll have a drink and go back to my room. Did you see the latest review of that SOB Koven? He's a true genius and the next great white hope."

"The last next great white hope was Jerry Cooney and that was fifty years ago."

"No, it was Larry Bird, the most underrated Hall of Famer that ever lived," Marty responded, his good humor restored by the specter of another drink and maybe the peanuts the waiter had brought.

I smiled and asked the waiter for two more drinks. We sat in companionable silence for awhile. Martin did silence better than anyone I knew.

"Your friend, Father ... Father? What was the guy's name? You know, the one trying to bring me back in the fold. I explained to him that I lost my faith years ago when I realized I didn't have faith, only a misnamed hope that I'd get what I wanted. That 'faith' kept me going for a long time. When I realized this, I lost my faith."

"Marty, I always thought you were Episcopalian."

"Oh, I am. Do you think I should have pointed it out? He seemed so excited by the prospect of saving me that it seemed mean-spirited to mention it."

There was something ferret-like about Marty. I've never trusted ferrets, even when they were old friends.

A man whom we hadn't seen in a long time came up and sat down—Theodore Hickey. He was the kind of guy that you were surprised to see even when you expected him.

"Hello, Pete. It's been too long," Theodore said.

"Theodore Hickey, as I live and breathe. What's this rumor about you being sober?" Marty said.

"Not a rumor. It's true and it's wonderful," the man said.

"Can I buy you a drink?" Marty said.

"I just told you, I'm not drinking."

"One drink never hurt anyone," Marty said.

"No, thanks."

"Oh that's right. I heard you were sober," Marty said.

"You're repeating yourself, Martin," I said.

"He always repeats himself. The alcoholic is like an actor in a play with the same lines he says over and over and over again—a different town, different venue, different cast, same story," Hickey said.

"The voice of sobriety breathing down my neck is none too pleasant a breeze," Marty said.

He left, neglecting to leave any money for his drinks.

"He doesn't want to hear the truth," I said.

Hickey got up and walked to a different table, saying, "To hell with the truth. It's not what anyone wants to hear."

I had a soft spot for Marty but he was skating close to the edge. He'd drop off soon enough. No matter how good a drinker you are, the booze will get you. Marty had been at the game a long time. He was on the verge of losing his job at the *Los Angeles Times*, and with that gone, he'd have no power. He'd made many enemies in his day.

I got up and followed after Martin, worried about him. Sometimes, if you drank long enough, often enough, a few drinks could finish you off. I was afraid he'd stroke out or have a heart attack.

Marty was standing in front of the restaurant, near the line of taxis. I walked up to him and said, "Say, friend. Do you want to come with me?"

He nodded. I signaled to the cab in front, which pulled up to us. I opened the door and helped Marty inside. Martin was sweating. He was shaking. His face was turning blue. I told the cabby to take us to Long Island College Hospital, which was about a mile away. I called the hospital and told the Emergency Room receptionist I had a patient in great distress, probably a heart attack, and that we'd be there in about ten minutes.

As we got out of the cab, he threw up. He clutched his left side. As I was bringing him inside, a triage team came running up to us pushing a gurney. They strapped Martin in, brought him inside and gave him oxygen and a shot. He was shuddering and shaking. I think he was having a seizure. Jesus.

Another ambulance pulled up, and some EMT's raced a man inside. I could not stop shaking. Shades of Iraq. I felt cold, sensing the angel of death flying over us. Poor Marty. He was a good guy and deserved better. He deserved better.

I stayed in his little cubicle in the ER. He had calmed down and was sleeping. A doctor came in and told me that Marty was suffering from acute alcohol poisoning. He woke Martin up and got him to sign some papers, although it was clear that Martin didn't have a clue what he was signing.

"The rehab will send a car for him as soon as he's fit to go. If not, I doubt he'll last three months. You've saved this man's life," the physician said.

What a joke. I was his good friend, maybe his only friend, and he and I had clinked glasses and drunk ourselves silly, even though I knew he shouldn't drink. I should have stopped him.

Siegel called my cell phone. He kept saying, "Nobody can stop a drunk from drinking but God."

I thought that was nice of Siegel. I appreciated the call.

I checked my watch. It was 10:30. I couldn't believe I had been in the hospital for four hours. I hailed a cab and went home.

I stopped the cabby at a corner bodega, since I wanted to buy a pack of Marlboro Lights. I heard a scream and saw two large men in an alley. A well-dressed man lay on the ground with his head split open. He was shaking, vomit and blood covering his mouth, face and neck, his trousers wet with his own urine. I saw skinny legs with black high heels sticking out from under a large man. I couldn't see her face. I heard muffled screams.

I could have kept walking. No one would ever have known except me, but that was enough. I picked up an old-fashioned coke bottle, half-empty and charged. I began swinging and I hit my first mark, breaking the bottle, spilling coke all over me. It felt good.

I swung, screamed, and yelled, not feeling the barrage of blows that rained on my body. I knew going in I had no chance. It didn't matter. A light from a flashlight bent into the alley. I heard a siren and the background noise of a police radio. The attackers ran.

I went home, exhausted, beaten and feeling wonderful.

Chapter 8

I limped into my building and found a Federal Express package left outside the mailbox. It was from the War Department, United States Army. I opened it and saw a letter and a Silver Star in a box with red velvet. The letter congratulated me on winning the medal. I read no more.

The war had ruined me. It had left me impotent, morally and emotionally. I wanted no memory of it, least of all a piece of tin signifying nothing. I stuffed everything back in the package. When I went up to my apartment, I threw the package into the garbage, next to two empty bottles of Jack Daniels and yesterday's racing form.

I soaked in the bath tub for a long time, reading a little of *Midnight in Peking*. I went to sleep easily and slept most of the night.

The next day my right hand was swollen. I felt pain under my left rib, and had bruises up and down my body. Nothing was broken.

I made some coffee and toasted a bagel. I read the morning paper and went on my way. It was a beautiful day, warm and sunny. I headed downtown to a ceremony I didn't want to attend.

It was the first time I had seen Ground Zero up close. Reporters, TV trucks, and smiling politicians milled about. I didn't want to be here. A stylish fellow, with a bad comb-over, wore a hard hat and held a shovel. The Mayor dug some dirt from a hole and made a speech. This was the beginning of a new era. We proved that we were still standing.

I found this rather unpleasant. I tried to look at these two men, who seemed to be enjoying themselves. I couldn't look at them. I pointed my camera and shot. I was crying so hard I was having trouble breathing.

They never found my brother's body, not even an arm or a leg or a piece of clothing. My mother decided to put his old hockey helmet and his favorite stick in the coffin. You should have your body buried when you die. People should be able to be buried in a coffin.

I took one very good shot. I caught a rainbow arcing from the brilliant sun as it reached downward to the earth, terminating in the soil where so many unclaimed lay dead.

As I headed home, I kept looking at the picture of the rainbow. I just wanted to lie down and go to sleep.

When I woke up, a note had been slid under the door from my neighbor, telling me that a woman had come by with a fat guy. The letter said they'd be back by six. It was now about eight.

I hung my pants up in the closet and poured myself a drink.

Dylan texted me to meet her at *il Mulino*. Like a dog to a bone, I washed up and went to meet her.

It was a four-star restaurant. I loved the pecan wood paneling on the walls, the lush tablecloths, the heavy sterling silver, and sparkling glassware. The carpets on the floor were so thick and rich that you felt like you were swimming in velvet. I sat at the massive polished mahogany bar, looking at the rows and rows of top shelf booze, underneath the wide mirrors. Once again, I was waiting for Dylan.

She walked in and announced, "The party can start. I'm here."

I got up and hugged her. She gave me a kiss that lasted an instant longer than I expected. "Dodo is taking us out for dinner," she told me.

"Dylan, I love you. Why can't it just be us?"

"Petey, darling, you're always my favorite," she told me.

"Why is somebody else always around?"

"Don't be mad at me. I can only help who I love, not who loves me."

Dodo walked into the restaurant, seemingly attended to by the headwaiter and several waiters. We were quickly seated at a table for six.

Dodo was very amusing. Dylan was quiet but laughed appreciatively. She asked questions that helped make Dodo shine, as though he needed that.

Charles, the head waiter, came over, seemingly unbidden and introduced himself to us. It was clear that Dodo was a valued customer. A minion brought over a bucket filled with ice, in which was a bottle of champagne.

The head waiter opened the champagne with a flourish and poured in into three beautiful champagne flutes. Dylan, Dodo, and I picked up the beautiful champagne goblets and sipped for a second. We stopped in amazement. This was very special indeed.

"Make a toast, Petey," Dylan said.

"To good wine," I said.

Dodo smiled.

"Yes," he said. "Enjoy the wine."

Dylan pushed her glass forward. "Let's enjoy more of this."

Charles bent over slightly and poured very slowly, a glass for each of us, and two for Dodo.

"I have found that I must be drunk to make the dull interesting," Dodo said.

"Is that an insult?" Dylan said.

"No, no. You're anything but dull," he said.

"I've no patience for the dull," Dylan said. "I'm surprised someone who's seen as much as you would waste your time with nobodies."

She wasn't drunk, but she was getting careless.

Dodo smiled ruefully. "My dear, I've been around forever, too long perhaps, but that is difficult to avoid after you've reached a certain age. I've made fortunes and I've lost fortunes. I've walked with kings and begged for food. I've had things happen to me that would have destroyed most men."

"We all have crosses to bear," I said.

She looked at Dodo. "You're in our little club."

I don't think I could afford the membership," he said.

"You don't have a choice. You're one of us or you're not one of us. It's how things work," she said.

"Dylan's rule," I said. "Enjoy the ride."

"That's right. Dylan's rule," Dylan said with a slight rasp in her voice, making her irresistible.

I watched her as she smiled and made herself smaller and more beautiful, her eyes larger and translucent, losing everything that was strident and discordant.

She put down her glass and did not drink any more.

Dodo looked at Dylan and then looked me in the eye and laughed, sharing our inability to do anything other than adore her. I liked the man. He was a throwback to a better time, when a handshake meant something.

It was a good party. We had come in late and were the only customers. The owner and two waiters, who acted as though it were early in the afternoon, betrayed not a hint of wanting to leave, it being, after all, a four-star restaurant.

I didn't see what Dodo left as a tip but judging from the response of the waiters, it had to have been an awful lot. He bought a bottle of hundred-year-old cognac, but Dylan was ready to leave and refused it with a modest smile. I wondered if this circumspection would last. I thought her need for alcohol would be too strong.

Dodo was beaming. He was happy.

Dodo savored the cognac, as did I. Dylan was careful not to spoil the mood. Soon, though, she became restless.

"Let's get out of here," Dylan said.

"As you wish. I am expecting a friend so shall remain here. Please take the car. Tiny, my driver, is at your disposal. This was a wonderful evening. It was my pleasure," Dodo said.

Dylan and I thanked him and left.

A very tall, very wide man, with coal black skin, wearing an impeccably well-tailored chauffeur's uniform stood beside a black Mercedes limo. He moved gracefully for a man of his girth.

"My name is Tiny," he said, with a self-deprecating smile. I 'm Dodo's driver . Please tell me where you want to go."

The man smiled a beautiful smile. I stood close to him and realized he smelled wonderful. I couldn't pinpoint the fragrance, but it was probably the best cologne I'd ever smelled.

We got into the big car. Tiny drove us to Dylan's hotel. She laid her head in my lap. Her hair covered her eyes. I gently brushed it away. I looked at her face and couldn't believe that anything that beautiful existed. The world stopped. I wanted to be lost in the moment forever. The next thing I knew, we were at the hotel. Time had betrayed me. Dylan accepted a chaste kiss and pushed me away. She got out of the car and walked away.

I had an idea and called her to come back.

I asked Tiny to take us to St. Michael's Cemetery in East Elmhurst, Queens, where my brother was buried. He had been a volunteer fireman in Ladder Ten, and spent his time in New York as a graduate student and fighting fires. He died on September 11th—on his third trip into a building he knew would collapse.

It was after midnight. The gates to the section where he was buried were locked. A gravedigger in a black suit with death tattooed on his face let us in. I gave him ten bucks and smiled at him warmly, but everything about him gave me a cold feeling inside.

It started snowing as we reached my brother's modest grave. His headstone was small and efficient. I thought of my parents, who had lost their first-born. They had met Dylan once. My mother said she had the look of a woman who caused great despair.

We sat on the ground in front of his grave. In the distance we could see white smoke coming from the chimneys of the houses surrounding the cemetery.

"This would make a great picture," I said.

Dylan said nothing.

In spite of all the tragedy that surrounded me, this was just an impotent man's pitiful attempt at seduction. Bringing

Dylan here was not about mourning. It wasn't about my brother at all. It was about Dylan, always Dylan, wanting her to love me.

"Dylan, do you have a pen?"

She handed me a pen and a piece of paper from her Chanel bag. I wrote. The truth was I had written it months before.

>*Snow buries earth. Soul silently regenerates, amassing glittering generalities and far-flung regret-no more, no more, only hypocritical time, recounting a multitude of foolish realities.*
>
>*Now this, now that, now nothing, and silently the snow still falls and the families glorify their dead and lament the living. We now clasp the past closely, and remember those who have departed— for a peace not known on earth. The snow is healing wounds and scars acquired long ago. Furnaces roaring, fire places aglow-as we attempt, slowly now, and in a rapidly growing frenzy, to forget the past and start again.*
>
>*That was then and this is now, and love can start at any time, if we just know how.*
>
>*So love we can and love we must, and never more do roam, and care for those about us still in our simple, peaceful home.*

"Dylan, what do you think?"

"It's beautiful. I wish I were a poet," she said.

The gravedigger returned. We got the hint. We trudged back to the car and trudged back to the City.

We went into another hot-happening club called Lava, with all its glamor and glitz. Dylan wanted to be a poet no more. She danced seductively with a beautiful blond woman in a gold sequined dress. I was mesmerized by the loose-fitting bodice of the stranger's dress, which revealed and covered her small perfectly formed breasts as she moved.

Cohen's ugly head reared once again. He looked so pathetic I almost felt sad for him.

"You two are always disappearing. It's getting tiresome," he said.

I said nothing, making a note to myself to remember what he'd said, in case I ever felt sorry for him again.

The rest of our crowd showed up, which gave me coverage to leave without saying good-bye to anyone.

Tiny was standing outside his limo and offered me a lift home. I sat in the front next to him as we drove.

I got out of the limo and thanked him. He drove off.

I walked up the steps, opened the door, and came inside.

I had no trouble falling asleep.

Chapter 9

The next few days were quiet. Dylan had disappeared from the scene, as had Dodo and Smith and Bernie. I didn't miss any of them. I had my work, eating with friends, getting some exercise, and sleep. I started writing my blog again for the first time in over a year.

I was so happy to be seeing my good friend Doug Gosling. He'd just returned from Boston, where he was lecturing on Nichomachean Ethics. I'd never seen him so chipper. He'd been told he was on a short list for a Nobel Prize in literature. Many people were starting to acknowledge him as the greatest living American author.

He stayed a day, and went to Prague. When he came back, we met at Pete's Tavern on Irving Place, and he told me of his travels.

"It was very peculiar. I started to make some whiskey sours. I remember that. Then it was time to come home. A lot happened, but I don't know what. There were some pictures on my phone, which were useful but upsetting. Apparently, I found some girl and we went hiking. I took about thirty pictures of scenery and people that were fuzzy. I'd been shaking the camera or maybe I had the shakes. Didn't have a clue who the people were, or if I knew them. Very disconcerting. I haven't had a drink since."

He held an open bottle of beer. I looked at him and at the bottle.

"I mean no hard liquor, a beer a day, and a glass of wine. I feel much better, even went to an AA meeting."

"How did that go?"

"Couldn't say. It was in Polish. Might go to some more if I start up again."

I thought about that and about drinking less. Things were really a lot better without the drinking.

"Let me tell you, Doug, it's been wonderful here. Quiet. No drama. I hate drama. I never realized it until I didn't have it any more. Been getting decent sleep and good food. I love it."

"I have to be a little more careful about how much I drink. No need to go cold turkey, just have to control it. I'm not an alcoholic—just a man who likes his booze."

I never thought that I was an alcoholic. I didn't even like the stuff. I drank to be sociable. Just got caught up in the scene. I hadn't any trouble these last weeks without drinking. I didn't even miss it.

We sat there in peaceful silence, congratulating ourselves on our temperate natures. I got a text from Dylan. Peace was coming to an end. She was around the corner.

I texted her to come by.

She walked up to the table.

"Oh my," said Doug. "Come join us." His eyes were lenses, taking in all the absurdity.

"Hello, hello, darlings. I just got back."

"Doug Gosling, my friend Dylan," I said." It's amazing you two have never met. Maybe that's because you're both always leaving."

They smiled as I said, "Come and eat with us."

"No time, I've got to take a shower."

"Have a drink first," I urged her.

Doug nodded his head in agreement. Somehow, we found ourselves enjoying Patrón, the world's most expensive Tequila, or maybe just the best. An image of Liza, smiling, floated across my consciousness and was gone.

Doug and I sat at the table panting, two dogs in heat, tied up and salivating, fighting for the slightest bit of attention.

Dylan was waiting for Alex, her true love of the moment. She'd come from a vacation that I doubt was solo, since I'd never known her to travel alone. I was sick of the dance, sick of the drama that never led anywhere, but I was paralyzed. Doug knew nothing about Dylan except that she was beautiful. If beauty were a red flag, Dylan was more of a conflagration.

She had freckles and no make-up on. She looked ten years younger than before she left. The time away had agreed with her. She was wearing jeans and a brown tweed blazer. Her hair fell down her shoulders in no particular style. She looked like the face of Chanel again.

"Listen, Alex is coming and Dodo wants to take us all out to dinner. I'll take a shower and be back in an hour," Dylan said.

"My darling, you are never any place in an hour," I told her.

"Sweetie, Dodo adores me, but I doubt his love would survive being kept waiting. Besides, Alex will be here as well, and it would be rude if I weren't here for him."

"I didn't think rudeness was a factor in any decision of yours."

"Oh Petey, don't be mean. I'll be back."

"You're always leaving when no one wants you to go," I said.

"That's what I'm famous for," Dylan said.

And off she went.

"That's one hell of a dame," Doug said. "God, she's beautiful. I have never seen a woman so beautiful."

The waiter came over, unbidden, with two whiskeys and soda, which we drank quickly. A man and a woman walked by. They had their arms around each other. The woman was quite pretty, but even the memory of Dylan was enough to make us not bother to look.

I motioned the waiter, almost without thinking, and he brought us more drinks. How little it took, I thought, for us to go back to our old ways. Music from the bar came to us softly:

> *"Yes, they're sharing a drink they call loneliness*
> *But it's better than drinkin' alone."**

---

*From "Piano Man" by Billy Joel

For some reason, the song made me feel sad. I was pleased when the music stopped. Doug and I each had another drink. Yes, sing us a song, piano man.

"What do you want to do?" I asked.

"Let's wait for the lady."

"And indeed she is a lady, a very fine lady. But she and punctuality do not even have a nodding acquaintance."

Sam, the manager, walked up to our table with a beautiful young girl next to him.

"Mr. Stanton, I don't mean to bother you, but this is Lexie, our weekend hostess. She'd really like to meet you."

She couldn't have been more than twenty. She had her whole life in front of her, which was a good thing. I sat there with Doug, taking her in.

"Your pictures are incredible," she told me.

She had come to New York to be a model. It was an old story but she was pretty so we asked her to sit down.

"You look familiar to me," she said to Doug. "You're famous, right. Are you the guy who landed the plane in the river where nobody died?"

"No, not really," Doug said.

"He's a great drinker," I offered.

"What made you decide to come to New York to become a model now?" Doug asked, ignoring my comment.

"My mom died, my dad didn't care what I did, so I left, not that my mom would have cared either," she said.

"How'd she die?" I asked.

"Heart attack. She was only forty years old," Lexi said.

"I'm a writer," Doug muttered. "Do you mind if I ask you a question?"

"No, not at all," she responded.

"If you could say anything to your mother right now, what would it be?"

"If she were on her death bed, I'd hug her and tell her I loved her. If she were young and healthy I'd tell her to fuck off."

"I'm going to put that in my next book," Doug said. "I'm Doug Gosling, the writer."

"Oh," she exclaimed, "You're still alive. I thought you died like fifty years ago."

That shut him up.

"If you want, I'll take some pictures for you. Modeling's a tough profession and you remind me of someone who broke my heart," I said.

"That's so sad," she said. "What happened?"

"I don't really know."

"Well I think she must be crazy. At least you found out before it was too late."

"It's never too late," Doug said. "You see, my dear. We forget those we love. It's those who didn't love us we remember."

"Let's change the subject," I said.

"No," Doug responded. "Regale her with tales of love lost and betrayal. Everyone I ever loved betrayed me. For years I thought it was me. Then I realized that's what people do."

"Do you still love her?" Lexi asked.

"Yes," I said.

"Well, then maybe it still has a chance," she offered.

Once again Doug interrupted. "Ah, the lover's deception. Always thinking you could do something to make her change how she felt. I quote myself: 'Indifference is the greatest aphrodisiac.'"

Doug was trying but she was ignoring him, probably not realizing that a famous writer could help her as much as I could.

Lexie bit her lip, reminding me of Dylan, bringing me back to an earlier time...

I had been standing on the beach as the sun rose. My heart fluttered. "You're more perfect than the sunrise," I whispered. She gave me that soft smile.

"I love you more than life itself," I told her.

She looked at me, her eyes so inviting, and replied, "I'm going to wear my white Dolce and Gabbana tonight. It doesn't make my hips look too big, right?"

That one moment summed up our entire relationship.

My thought was interrupted by Doug saying "Petey, you know Senator Eisbrouch?"

"Yes. How are you, Senator?"

"Great, but running late for a fundraiser."

He shook everyone's hand twice and left, presumably to shake more hands.

"You know Senator Eisbrouch well?" she asked.

"I dated his third wife. She was the ideal third wife, pretty, willing, and stupid," Doug said.

Lexi looked at Doug with one of those looks that told him he had no chance with her. It didn't stop him.

"Does your father help you as you try to find fame and fortune?"

No," she said. "He wouldn't, even if he could."

"Let's drink a toast to lousy parents. I now quote myself once again: 'They were gone or died, which was the best thing I could say about them'."

She laughed. "You're funny."

She had a nice laugh. I took her face in. She got prettier as I got drunker.

"I have to go,' Lexi said. "Will you really take my picture?"

"I certainly shall," I said. "Give me your number."

She wrote her number on a napkin. Underneath it she wrote 'I'm up for anything.'

"I love the young and innocent," Doug said as she departed.

I handed him the napkin. He laughed hard and ordered two more bourbons.

I took my sweater off and settled in. I asked for a double shrimp cocktail and clams casino. We were in it for the long haul. A few people approached the table to ask for Doug's autograph or tell him how much they loved his books.

Doug basked in his success. Yes, being famous and making money, maybe a lot of it, gave confidence to any man, sort of like being beautiful gave confidence to almost any woman.

Doug and I sat there drinking for hours. We enjoyed the mild buzz, the best buzz, when alcohol was still being kind and hadn't taken over.

Dylan sent me a text that she'd be at the restaurant in a minute. We settled up and went outside.

A big limo slowed as it approached the café. It stopped.

Tiny, for it was he, immaculately attired as usual, climbed out of the car. He held the door while Dylan, Alex, and Dodo stepped out.

Alex hurried over to us. "Doug Gosling, as I live and breathe. It's been too long, my old friend."

Doug looked at him warily.

At our last meeting, Alex had been puffy and looked like a middle-aged, not very attractive man. He now seemed taller and thinner, with fine bone structure, and a lovely smile.

"Hello, Petey, it's good to see you. You're looking well," Alex said.

"As are you, Alex Bank. You're Dorian Grey."

"I'm a hearty believer in a team of plastic surgeons, and Mommy and I get a two-for-one discount."

"Dodo," I nodded to the big man. "This is my friend, Doug Gosling."

"I am honored to meet you, good sir."

"This is so boring. It's as though I never went away. I feel as if I'm waiting to wake up—like Sleeping Beauty," Dylan said.

"Not really," I said, "As it happens, we've all been busy. I've been taking pictures of both young and old boxers for *Sports Illustrated*."

"The fight?" Alex looked up. "Now those chaps are frightfully fit. It would be good to see the fight. A true fight between champions."

Dodo nodded to Tiny, standing in view, who started talking on his cell phone. Tiny finished his conversation and nodded to Dodo.

"Yes," Dodo said. "I have tickets for us all. What a fine idea, Alex, a very fine idea," Dodo said. "Let's see the fight, shall we?"

"I've heard enough about fights to last me ten years," Dylan said. "I do believe Siegel is going to the fight, which is enough to keep me here."

"And I as well," Alex Bank added. "He sounds like quite an ass."

"No," said Dodo, "he fights too well for that. Don't ever underestimate a man who has a knockout punch."

I wondered how he knew about Siegel. I was to learn that Dodo knew everything about whatever he deemed important.

Dodo shook his head. "We've got to get going. We shouldn't be late. Fights are always best seen with friends, I believe. So do come."

Things were arranged before anyone could say no. I'm not sure that I was so inclined. I told Dodo I already had tickets for the fight and that Douglas was coming along.

But for the rest of them? How much easier life is with a lot of money. You don't have to sing for your supper. Sing that song, piano man. Anything is better than drinking alone.

We were in New York. We were going to an old-fashioned prizefight—the dancer, fluid and graceful, against the puncher. The dancer was the heavy weight champion of the world. The puncher had once been the champ, but five years is a lifetime in the fight game.

We ran into Siegel as we walked into the aging fighter's dressing room.

"Hey, ESPN, my favorite photographer, you always make me look good," the pugilist said, recognizing me.

"How are you doing, Mike?" I asked him.

"You seen this guy?" he says.

"Just in the gym."

"Well," Mike said, "I wish they didn't test for juice. Then I'd kill him."

"Come on, Mike, you're the champ. You done this before. You hit hard. You're hard to hit," Hendo said. Hendo was his cut man. They went back a long way.

"I'm a very bad man," the champ said.

"He looks easy to hit," I said.

"Easy for you to say when you're sitting in the stands. You couldn't knock him out with a baseball bat," Hendo said.

"Sure," Mike said, "Ten years ago I'd have knocked him out in the first round."

"Yeah, but he be like twelve years old," Hendo said.

"Come on, Champ. You're the best," Bernie told him.

"I really would have kicked his ass back then. This is going to be one long night," Mike said.

"Think positive. Think positive," Hendo said.

We were in a dressing room that smelled of failure and fear and disappointment. It smelled of giving up.

Hendo looked at us and said, "That's it, folks. Time to go. Enjoy the show. We're gonna shock the world."

The rest of the entourage was in the room and quiet.

The time had come for us to depart, so we did.

"He seems to like you a lot," Siegel said.

"We get along well," I said.

"He doesn't like many people. He's cold. He always was decent to me, even when he was champ. He thought I was classy because I went to Princeton."

"At least he heard of the place."

"He's tough and he has a lot of experience," Doug said.

"The smart money's on the champ," I said. "I like Mike, though. He's a stand-up guy."

We went to our seats. It was the usual dog and pony show—very tall black men in mink coats; women glossy, velvety, and beautiful with large breasts defying gravity and small waists and smooth skin, like exotic birds never found in nature.

We missed the prelims, which was a mistake because there were some good fighters from the old Soviet bloc. The lights went down. A fire fighter who had survived 9/11 sang the National Anthem badly. We all cheered him mightily. The two warriors entered the ring. They ratcheted up the excitement level, even for a fight like this, which was probably a tank job.

Mike was a Palooka, but he was no dummy. He had a real knockout punch. I doubted he'd last two rounds. I hoped for his sake that he wouldn't be too brave. Punch like the man he used to be for a few rounds, then take it on the chin and leave with a big payday.

If it went down any other way, the fix would have to be in. Not so easy to do these days. Not like the old days. These days it was all business. Sad really, the romance was gone.

Everyone wanted their thirty pieces of silver—or their ten million bucks.

The fight started out with Mike punching hard with body shots, keeping close in so the Champ couldn't use that long reach. Mike stayed in the clinches as long as he could, and lasted five rounds.

Dylan was screaming. She was rooting for the Champ. He was too pretty not to love. The fans were rooting for both of them, but fans can be like that. It was an action packed five rounds. The fans got their money's worth. For about a round or two, it looked like Mike would pull it off.

He stepped back, and the Champ smashed a right to Mike's chin. His head snapped back. He really got tagged. He crumpled, just crumpled. He was down, and he was out. One, two, three, four, five, six, seven, eight, nine, ten, it was over. Yup, experience tells. Mike made it a great fight, a crowd pleaser. That takes a lot of experience.

Mike looked pretty beat up. The Champ was a modern day Mohammed Ali, fast, graceful, and very powerful. His jabs had done damage, but to the body, not the brain, to the body but not the kidneys or spleen. Mike protected himself, and the Champ was a gentlemen. They both made it look like a helluva fight, like in the old days when both fighters would be half-dead at the end, winner and loser alike.

They kept showing the knockout punch and Mike's head snapping back. You knew it was over. Mike was a real pro. He had a good payday. He could move to some third world country and live like a king.

I was glad. He'd gotten screwed plenty on his way up. Now he was getting a nice ride on his way down.

Chapter 10

Doug and I tacitly agreed not to look for the Dylan brigade or call to see where they were. We snuck out of one of the rear exits and found the whole gang getting into Dodo's limo.

Dylan summoned us into the car with a wave of her hand. "Why didn't you answer your cell phone?" she asked.

"Well, we're here. Where are you going? I asked.

Alex said to some joint in Brooklyn.

We sped downtown and ended up in Williamsburg, a part of Brooklyn near the Manhattan Bridge. We smelled the garlic as we got out of the car. The place was jammed, with an hour wait, but an elderly gentleman, impeccably dressed, with deep blue eyes immediately escorted us to a table.

He shook hands with Dodo and nodded his head at the rest of us.

Two beautiful young girls, eighteen if we were lucky, or a lot less, ran over to Dylan. The girls were gorgeous, but you could see the difference between them and Dylan, like thoroughbreds at the Kentucky Derby and all the rest of the horses. The waiter placed a little table next to the bigger table and two chairs next to it, so swiftly and quietly that you would have thought the girls had been there the whole time.

Of course, we learned all about them, two private school beauties here with an aunt who had left quietly. They laughed about it. Dear auntie was the younger sister of a second, much younger wife, and was barely older than they.

Dodo looked over at the blue-eyed man and gave a funny look. The guy shrugged.

When the *maitre'd* came over to the table, he suggested that we put ourselves in his hands.

"Not a problem. The wines?"

"The owner would like you to be his guests, sir. I promise you the wines will be more than satisfactory. I suggest you start with a special aperitif. It will enhance your dining pleasure."

Doug asked for scotch.

"Certainly, Mr. Gosling," the maitre'd said. "Your pleasure."

He left quickly.

"I don't think that went over too well. I guess we're supposed to take whatever is offered and let it go at that. Say, Dodo, do you know what kind of place this is, or who the blue eyed guy is, for that matter?" Doug asked.

"He is the friend of a dear friend of mine, Doug. Shall we say no more?"

It was interesting to me that words said by a smiling Dodo, polite and kind, could have such force. I was content to say no more.

We hadn't eaten much that day or the day before. I was hungry.

A waiter came over and gave us special wine glasses. Another poured from a bottle that had no label. He put a bit into Dodo's glass. Dodo held the glass to his nose and sniffed. He took a sip and clearly enjoyed the drink.

This was the most animation Dodo had exhibited.

The waiter filled Dodo's glass.

"It is satisfactory?" he asked.

Dodo laughed. "Please inform our host that this is more than superb."

I noticed that the waiter filled our glasses from a different bottle, one with a label that denoted a fine vintage Port. Another waiter came with various appetizers—raw oysters and clams, cooked clams, calamari, and a fried cheese with anchovies that was phenomenal.

The conversation was strange. It was as though we were all experts and willing to share our knowledge. No one listened to anyone else, but we did enjoy talking.

As soon as we tasted the food, we stopped speaking. The two nymphets giggled, but it was background music. Dylan ignored them. The rest of us were entranced. It didn't seem to bother Dylan, who asked a waiter for vodka. He brought it promptly. He also put a large red wine glass before every place and filled it with a special Amarone Classico, one of my favorites. The little girls were happy with some white wine.

Three waiters made a big production of putting some pasta with butter on each plate, sprinkling something on the top, and serving it as though it were gold.

"This is so good," said Dylan, digging in.

I remembered a night in Paris at a four star restaurant when Dylan was eating with her fingers. I had found it enchanting. A splendid night in Paris—my memories were lovely—but the pictures were blurred. They weren't right. No, the pictures were right and the memories wrong. I started telling Dylan about it.

She said, "Sometimes facts ruin memories. Forget them."

Dodo paid no attention to our sidebar. "White truffles always are exquisite, particularly Tartufo Bianco, from Piedmont," he said.

Harper, one of the young girls, sculpted out of rosy marble with not a flaw on her skin and beautiful brown eyes and blond hair, looked up at him.

"Uh, I think these are from the Marche region near Aqualanga. The best truffles come from there, "she said.

She looked up at me. She grinned that "I hate it that people think I'm a dope and are so condescending" smile.

Dodo beckoned the *maitre'd*. "This is special."

"Yes," said the man, "these were just flown in from Italy this morning—from Aqualanga."

Dodo nodded to the girl. His smile widened.

"Did you enjoy the fight?" he asked.

"Oh, yes," the girl replied. "He fought great for an old guy. I wanted him to win, but that wasn't going to happen."

Dodo paused for a second and asked her if she knew who the last heavyweight champion had been.

She looked at Dodo and recited the last three champs. Then she got up from the table and asked her friend and Dylan to come with her to the bathroom. Dylan refused. The two girls went off together. Dodo smiled affably but stared after the girl as though he were memorizing her face.

The rest of the food was beautifully cooked and the wines splendid. We were all more than a little drunk when we got up from the table. Mr. Blue Eyes escorted us to the front door.

Dodo expressed his thanks. "I don't think I have ever had a better meal. Superb."

The owner bowed. "It was my pleasure to serve you."

"I hope I have the opportunity to return the favor," Dodo said.

By this time, the rest of us had stopped trying to be polite. We were bit players and had no speaking parts—but it was a great meal.

Dodo seemed distracted. Knowing the dangers of deducing facts from limited knowledge, I was not disposed to think the Aqualanga truffles would have disconcerted him, but he was a strange fellow.

I had a strong feeling that the little beauty should remove herself from his presence post-haste.

He smiled at her. "So you model?"

She smiled back, sweetly, and said, "No, not really—I'm a junior in high school."

"Would you want to model?" he asked.

"If I looked like Dylan I'd model," she replied. "I swim. It takes up a lot of time." She smiled at Dodo and closed her eyes. She was an interesting girl, shrewd, smart, or very stoned.

And so the night passed.

We got into the limo without saying a word. The car drove off.

"This has been a wonderful evening, Dodo. Fantastic fight. Fantastic food. Thank you for everything."

I noticed Dodo holding the hand of Harper's friend. The two of them had identical eyes, inky black and impenetrable.

I thought of the man someone had called Jimmy Blue Eyes, whose eyes were blue and twinkling and no more accessible. Shark's eyes.

I was a minnow swimming in a pool of sharks. It was time to get out of the pool.

"Enjoy your fishing. My friend set up a condo for you. It will be available in a few days. You will have the best accommodations with the most enjoyable conveniences on Montauk. I'll email all the information. Use whatever you find in the condo, the drinks, the wine, and the food. You can find no better fishing on this entire coast," Dodo said.

"I hope that I'll be able to repay your hospitality," I said.

"Your friend not writing about me is payment enough," Dodo said.

"Even if it were flattering?" Doug asked, laughing.

"I do keep a low profile, you know," Dodo said.

The limo stopped in the meatpacking district, in front of the Gansevoort Hotel. Alex, Doug, Dylan, Harper, and I got out. We went inside, and up to the rooftop. It was after two, but the pool was open because a wedding had run late.

The view was spectacular although the scene was muted. The moon had set, and the sun had not yet risen.

I looked at Dylan, thinking that this was a moment outside of time.

I said, "Dylan, don't move."

I pulled my camera out. I posed Dylan staring into the ominous sky, Doug a few feet away, wearing his fedora, gazing at her. I was thinking it was beauty staring at beauty— absolutely breathtaking, enchanting, casting a spell on all who watched.

Alex said, "It's like the sun's not going to rise."

Dylan shook her head, "No, Aristotle said that the sun always rises, and that there would always be a tomorrow."

Alex looked at her, annoyed, "Aristotle also said only silence gave the proper grace to women."

I put my camera away, took my shoes and socks off, and dipped my feet in the pool. I heard JZ and Alicia Keyes singing *Empire State of Mind*.

The pool was open winter and summer, but generally not this late. A lone waiter manned the barbecue grill in a private garden floating over Manhattan. I saw lights of cars driving by down below in a haze of moon glow, a magical time when all things seemed possible. The thing about Manhattan is that everything is always available, day or night or at four in the morning.

We didn't need food. I wanted cold water, coffee and an aspirin. Best way to prevent a hangover.

Alex went to the bathroom with Doug. Dylan, Harper and I sat at a large table.

"Have a nightcap instead?"

I groaned. "Well, maybe."

"I haven't had a chance to talk to you since we came to New York."

"No."

"Peter, how are you?"

"Fine," I said.

I wasn't fine. The drinking got to me and the tension and the secrets—and the lies. "I want to get some fishing in. I don't think I can take any more of this."

Dylan looked at me with a hard gaze. "By any chance is Bernie Siegel coming with us on this fishing trip?"

"Yes. What difference does it make?"

"He's a glutton for punishment," she said. "And it isn't attractive."

"What are you talking about?"

"Who do you think I spent my vacation with?" she asked me. She was careless, a Fitzgerald heroine. It wasn't pretty.

Seeing her in action took the bloom off the rose. I'd had enough of her and enough of her friends. I wanted to get away.

"Couldn't you have found someone better to amuse you?"

"My, you're getting spiteful. It doesn't become you."

"I don't care who you go on vacation with. I don't spend all my time thinking about you."

"I'm all you think about," Dylan said.

"That's not true."

"It doesn't matter what I do. Nothing will ever change," she said, smiling a little smile that once would have brought tears to my eyes. Her large eyes looked into mine. I saw her face, her beautiful face. One more time I forgot. One more time I loved her.

Harper had been texting all the while, ignoring us— ignoring her.

Dylan was popping pills. So was Harper. MDMA's and Ketamine washed down with champagne. They ordered Krystal.

Out of the blue, little Harper turned to Dylan and said matter of factly, "Do you mind if I fuck your boyfriend?"

Dylan asked me, "Do I mind?"

She turned to Harper and said, "Since you were polite enough to ask, how can I say no?"

Dylan gave her big belly laugh and said loudly, 'Knock yourself out."

Harper, maybe four inches shorter than Dylan, with a lot smaller chest, giggled.

"Thanks," she said. She was adorable.

Dylan, and Alex, who had been snorting Coke in the bathroom, left to go see some special DJ at 'Catch.' Doug grabbed a cab to his hotel. Harper and I walked the block to my rent-controlled apartment. I could have sublet it when I was out of the country, but I liked the freedom of knowing I had a place to come back to.

The young girl walked with me. My cell phone rang. I ignored it. It beeped. Dylan texted me. I didn't read it. Dylan's charms were wearing thin.

Harper and I walked up the five flights to my apartment. I unlocked the door. We went inside. It was small, maybe seven hundred and fifty square feet, with a kitchen, decent-sized bed, a living room with a desk, a table, and a chair. I stored almost everything I owned in a storage unit, or on line, easily retrievable.

The girl went to the bathroom and came out a few minutes later, naked. She was gorgeous, with a body craving sex. She lay down on the bed, an Odalisque.

"Are you over seventeen?" I asked.

"Oh, please," she said.

She turned over and moved her body suggestively, slowly and gracefully. If I could have performed, nothing would have stopped me.

"Dylan sort of suggested that you couldn't..."

"Sweet of her, but she's not a woman to be trusted."

"The war?"

"The war, morals, take your pick. Maybe you should go home."

"No problema. I'll sleep here. Do you have an Ambien?"

"How would that mix with all the stuff you've taken tonight?"

She shrugged.

"So, do you have one?"

I said no.

She rummaged around in her pocket book, pulled out a bottle of Ambien, and took two. She swallowed them without water.

I shook my head. "How'd you know where the truffles were from?"

"My folks have a villa in Italy. I have been wooed with truffles."

She climbed onto my bed and stretched herself out like a cat, lying next to me without an iota of self-consciousness.

She looked at me very sweetly.

I turned away.

"You're not going to do this?"

"No," I said. "I can't."

"That is so sad," she said.

We lay there without speaking for a few minutes. I looked at her. With her eyes closed, she looked peaceful and innocent. I couldn't help myself. I started to cry, not knowing why.

She opened her eyes and asked, "Are you okay?"

"Do you really care?"

She thought for about five seconds and said, "No, not really."

"Neither do I," I lied.

When I awoke the next morning, she and my medicine cabinet were gone. Good thing I'd hidden my pain pills, be hard to function without them. Dylan's little games returned to haunt me. I was filled with an unrelenting sickness in my soul.

Chapter 11

I went to the bathroom and threw up. I had to get away. Fishing was a good idea. Fishing had a purity to it, but we couldn't go to Montauk yet. We had arranged that Doug and I would take a train out to Montauk the following week, or would rent a car and drive to Dodo's friend's place. The rest of them would follow the next day. I emailed the address, as well as careful directions. The place was at the tip of Long Island and had spectacular fishing.

I spent the day taking pictures of the spectacular magnificence of Manhattan.

I didn't want to be drunk all the time, but it was getting to be a habit. When I was drunk, I didn't care if my world wasn't real. It wasn't that anything had changed. I just didn't care. I ended up in a dark bar. All the bars were dark. The well-lit ones went broke.

That night I went from bar to bar, club to club, until four o'clock in the morning. With luck, I wouldn't get home until the sun rose. The room was spinning, but I knew the trick of staring at a wall until it stopped.

See, it's easy to be tough when the sun is shining. I didn't want to go to bed because you get soft when you're home alone. You're still drunk, but the mantel of indifference is gone. You've lost the magic.

Suicidal ideation appeared at four-o'clock. I recognized it for the fraud it was. The thought of killing myself was mental masturbation, helping me get through the night. It's like your old friend's pretty wife. I might take her to dinner, but I sure as hell wouldn't bring her home.

That night, I wasn't sure what was going on. I was in a murky place that was all smoke. Sometimes the painkillers made me hallucinate. I saw things that weren't there. If I was lucky, they were benign. Once in a while, horrifying creatures filled my room, grabbing at me, trying to drag me to hell.

I hadn't told Dylan what was going on, just that I was sick, and that it was nothing serious. Between her drinking and her pills, she would forget. I thought I saw her in my bedroom, but I couldn't be sure.

"I'd love a drink—a Kir Royale," I told her.

"How about some lukewarm vodka with no ice?"

"Okay," I said.

"But if you're sick, you shouldn't be drinking," she said.

"It's good for me," I told her.

What was good for me was that the pain had stopped. The worry went away with the pain, not that I thought everything would be okay, just that it would be over. I was tired. I thought I'd been fighting the good fight, bravely, but my time was coming.

I didn't have much time left and nothing to do with it. The whimper and the bang, I thought. For me, the world ended with a yawn.

Dylan had some place to go. She left, if she'd been there at all.

Morning came later than usual. I always felt better in the morning. I could lie to myself when the sun was shining, but not in the middle of the night when the big screen of memory couldn't be turned off, when I had to face myself and my failures.

I had spent five years trying to fight self-pity and despair, but it was getting harder. The pain wore me down. It wasn't being sick, which was bad enough. It was everything else. I used to be brave. Now I was a frightened child, pretending to be fearless, but it was a hoax, a joke.

I couldn't pretend in my bed. I had no dreams, only nightmares. The days stretched before me in endless pain and despair.

I took a hot shower, a cold shower, had a Bromo Seltzer and three cups of strong coffee. It was enough to get me going.

I had a long day in front of me. I planned to visit my father's grave. I hadn't been there in two years and that was too long. My father was buried in Arlington Cemetery. He'd been a helicopter pilot in Viet Nam.

I was going back—to say a better goodbye to the man I loved more than any other. When he died, I lost my moral compass. When he died I began to drink without stopping. When he died, I died as well.

I emailed my friends to let them know I was going to be away for a few days. I let ESPN know that I would be unable to take any jobs for a few weeks. I received few responses. I needed to get away, to be anyplace but here.

I rented a car and drove toward Virginia. It was good getting out of the City, good driving mindlessly on the Jersey Turnpike. It was good to grab coffee from a ubiquitous Starbucks and good not to drink. It was good to listen to music that my friends would ridicule.

It was easier not drinking when I was alone. I wanted to get away from Dodo and Alex and Tiny and limos. I thought that maybe I'd be able to reconstitute, get centered, and simplify my life. Maybe I was leaving because I didn't want to see that man in the mirror. I had looked at him long enough and he wasn't a pretty sight.

The good times lasted, say, until later that night. I spent the time renting a car, and driving down south. I think there had been construction and a bad accident somewhere before Baltimore.

I saw cars stretched out for miles before me and behind me, a fitting symbol for the pilgrimage I was making. Nothing was moving. It was late and I decided to find a place to stop for the night.

I exited the Turnpike and drove on some small road in Maryland until I hit a motel colony beside a bay. I was surprised to find the little cottages expensive. The little room was small and not very clean but was convenient not only to the water but also to a cozy-looking bar.

I took a short shower, in a dingy stall with tiles missing, grout moldy and emanating a sickly smell. I dressed and went to the bar, which was grubby enough and poorly lit enough to be comfortable. They served hamburgers. I had one. It was good. I ordered a beer and figured I would have a few.

Two women in their forties, ridden a little hard but not bad, came up to the table. I invited them to sit down. I ordered a bottle of Chianti—or two. It went down easy.

We talked about whatever people talk about when they have nothing to say, but are trying to make a good impression. I had nothing to gain. That didn't make me stop trying.

"I think I'm good for one more bottle of wine," I said, and ordered Chianti.

I had a buzz on.

Good sense prevailed. I got up.

"This has been fun," I said. "I've got to get up early tomorrow, so thanks all and goodnight."

I saw the bartender looking at me as though he wanted to say something.

A couple walked out with me, standing a little too close.

"No need to walk me home," I said. "I'm right over there."

I gestured to my little shack, which was within walking distance. The man and woman walked off slowly.

I heard a line flapping in the breeze. When you're near a sailboat, you always have to tie down a strap that's loose. The odds are it would make no difference. The boat would sail at the same speed. Nothing untoward would happen, but everyone knows you tie down a flapping line.

I walked to the door and unlocked it. I felt them behind me. The man pushed me inside. The woman slipped in after us. She shut the door.

The man grabbed me. I guess I looked like a patsy. I remembered Dodo saying not to underestimate a man with a knockout punch. I wished I had one.

I grabbed at the guy, who was big but flabby. His eyes were dark. His face was still. For the first time, in the stillness and menace of his face, I realized the situation might be dangerous. He jabbed a few times, my face, my eyes, my gut. I fell because his punches were strong and sharp.

I was down on the floor. He was kneeling on my chest, still punching those short, sharp jabs. I thought he'd kill me after all. All the time I was looking for a weapon, anything.

I had a friend in the hospital back when I was first injured. They gave him a new liver. It was rough going. I said I wouldn't have a transplant, no matter what. It would be too hard.

He told me that you didn't know what you would do until the time came. You either fought for your life or you didn't.

I looked at the woman. She had the same light in her eyes I'd seen when Dylan cheered the prizefighter on. The guy smelled my blood. He was choking me. He banged my head against the floor as if it were a hammer and the floor were the nails.

This wasn't a cheap rental, but no one had cleaned it in a long time. I saw a screw driver under the table. I grabbed for it and held it tightly in my hand. I could scarcely breathe. I felt like I had about two more seconds of life.

I had the screw driver in my hand and shoved it into the soft flesh of his belly. Blood spurted out. The woman screamed. She ran out the door. She might have been going for help. He limped after her, holding the wet towel close to his stomach that I had thrown on the floor after my shower.

I kept gasping for breath. I saw a half-empty bottle of cheap vodka and drank the whole thing. I walked outside and sat on a rickety rocking chair on the little porch in front of my cottage. I wasn't thinking straight.

I fell asleep or passed out. The sound of rain woke me up. It was still dark. I didn't see any lights. The moon was shining weakly through dark and menacing clouds. The water kept slapping against the boats in the little marina.

The pale sun rose in the black sky. A black cloud of birds in a moving mass of beating wings hovered over the boats. I shivered, thinking that I could easily have walked to the water and fallen in, silently slipping to a watery grave.

My laugh was bitter. It was not a blessing to survive. I was not blessed, alive or dead.

The mass of birds flew higher in the air. The water was clearer. The bleakness of the storm gave way to a brilliant sun, painting pink, orange, and coral clouds.

Blood stained my shirt and my shoes. The psycho could have killed me and disappeared back into his life. He might have died. He might have stolen my car and driven away. If he had killed me, his lady friend wouldn't have said anything. I liked to think if he had killed her, I would have said something.

The flapping of wings, which signified the birds' departure, roused me from my paralysis.

I decided to write a blog about my father. Today was his birthday, probably my real reason for coming down here.

> *My father died on the same day he was born. He was efficient like that. He was my hero—not a hero who saved a town in a war or discovered a cure for a horrible disease. He was a man who did his best every day. He always had a smile and a kind word for anyone who crossed his path.*
>
> *He was a good father and a good man. When he got sick, I gave him my kidney. It was the most selfish thing I ever did. It gave me another year of smiles and laughs with my old man.*
>
> *Dad, I miss you so much.*

It was time. I showered, shaved, and put on clean clothes. I was ready to go to Arlington and face the dead. It was so early that there was no traffic. I swiftly reached my destination.

In Arlington National Cemetery were many heroes, some sung, some unsung. I walked among the well-kept graves, the small gravestones, the monuments to a country once proud and true.

I reached my father's grave.

"I'm sorry I haven't been here for so long. I never stop thinking of you, but I just get caught up in life. When I was young and didn't know what to do, I'd always think—what would my father do, and do the right thing. I stopped doing that some time ago.

"Life for me has become very difficult. I love a woman who's nothing like mom. She's careless, whimsical, unstable. I don't even know if she's capable of love, but Dad, I love her. Funny how different your one love is from mine but when you're in love, all women are the same—perfect."

I sat on the grass for maybe an hour, thinking of my old man and how lucky I had been to have him. I felt serene.

I miss you so much, I thought, as I got up. I walked off and tripped slightly.

I saw a stone with a woman's name. The girl had been seventeen when she died. I didn't know her. I had never seen her face. She was a stranger. I didn't know why or how she died. She was dead. The reason why didn't matter. It was some war and the war was over, as was her life.

I walked on, no longer at peace, no longer hearing the whispers of my father, a loving man content with his life.

I returned the car at the airport and flew back home on the shuttle. I ended up in New York, in my apartment and slept for fourteen hours straight. The bruises faded. The pain in my throat subsided. It was back to sitting in bars for hours, getting drunk, staggering home, and falling into deep, unsatisfying sleep.

Chapter 12

Doug and I took an early train from Penn Station. We travelled through Queens, not the garden spot of the world. The late nights and heavy drinking had gotten to us. We were feeling sluggish and slow. We had to change at Jamaica and almost missed the connecting train.

As we got onto the train for the final leg of our journey, Doug and I sat across from each other in an otherwise empty car. I fell asleep. I never dreamt but I was suddenly back in Iraq, so I must have been dreaming. I was in the Al/Anbar province, sitting in the back of a truck with six marines from Detachment One, speeding down a dark road in the middle of the night.

I was in the Army, early in my first tour of duty. My assignment was to shoot pictures of the rescue of a Canadian Journalist by the six Marines huddled close to me. These were serious men, here to do serious business.

I could hear the iPod of the Marine lieutenant next to me through his headphones, blasting John Lennon's song *Imagine*. Every time he got to an "aha" or an "ooh-hoo," the marine tilted his head back, closed his eyes, and sang along.

No one seemed to notice or care. The irony of the song was of no consequence to the warriors. This was a dangerous mission. Death was a part of the job, like a secretary answering a phone.

I took my camera out to take a picture of the men. A sergeant, who had done numerous tours of duty in Iraq, Afghanistan, and Yemen glanced at me, silently telling me that they didn't want medals and they didn't need fame. So no pictures.

I got it. I felt like one of them. As the symphony of war got closer, the lieutenant barked out orders. Two marines were getting their equipment ready.

"Oorah," one said.

"*Semper fi*," I retorted.

"*Carpe diem*," said the lieutenant with a deep laugh. "Stay close to me, kid. I'll keep you alive."

Suddenly, it wasn't so lonely and dark outside. The other Marines laughed as much at my presumption as at the kindness of this hardened Marine.

I felt myself coming out of my dream, waking up. I wanted to be back in the dream, back in the safety of my truck.

I opened my eyes and was in Montauk. I hated the feeling of being caught between two worlds, alienated from both and understanding neither. Slowly the murkiness lifted.

It was a lovely day. We walked to the Montauk Playhouse Community Center for our fishing permits. Parts of Montauk were beautiful, parts singularly dismal.

The Community Center was a modern facility that housed the annex for the Town Clerk, the office that provided fishing, beach, and parking permits. A chipper little woman, at least in her seventies, had our permits ready in minutes. She handed me a large manila envelope and a handful of brochures touting attractions in the area.

"Any place we could get a drink that also has some food?" Doug asked.

"I know just what you're looking for. The Sloppy Tuna Restaurant is very scenic. It's the only waterfront bar in the area. Good food and every drink is a double," she said with a little smile.

The restaurant was light, airy, and very quiet. It was chilly, so we sat inside facing a bathroom. No, it wasn't Paris, where every vista was a delight to the eye, and every meal a gustatory celebration. It was something better—it was home.

A waitress came over to us. She was young and appealing and wore a button that said, "Hi, my name is Lindsey. The third one's on me." She smiled as she placed menus in front of us.

"Could I have Stoli on the rocks, with a twist of lime for my vitamin C, please?" Doug asked, smiling at the pretty face.

"I'll have the same," I said.

"Do you want anything to eat?" she asked.

"Bring us some oysters," Doug said. "We're here to do some fishing. Any recommendations?"

"*Rod and Reel* said we had the best surf fishing and fly casting in the world," she said. "Joey, the bus boy over there, can tell you a lot better than I can."

"Thank you so kindly," said Doug. Douglas was always polite to attractive women.

Lindsey smiled. She walked over to Joey and spoke to him.

"She is certainly pretty," Doug laughed. "I'd marry the hell out of her."

"Would you really get married again?" I asked.

"Well, hunger can only be satiated by food, temptation by sex, and happiness by marriage. So, no, I'm not going to get married again," Doug said.

A tall and gangly kid walked to the table. He was about eighteen or nineteen. He introduced himself as Joey. "What kind of fishing are you gentlemen looking for?"

"We're open. Something simple, without a lot of gear, and won't take hours to get to," I said.

"But with a challenge," Doug interrupted. "It should be interesting."

Joey nodded. "Have you done any surf fishing? I promise it will be remarkable."

"Fine," I said, waiting for him to tell me it was the best in the western hemisphere.

"It's good to start early," he said. "How about if I pick you up at 7:00 tomorrow morning?"

We sorted out the particulars, what gear he would provide, how much it would cost, and how long we would be fishing.

The kid had a facile brain and was economical with words. Doing business with him was a pleasure.

I asked if he needed a deposit. He laughed. "I think you're good for it," he said. Joey shook our hands firmly and left.

The waitress brought our drinks, silverware, and water. She was efficient and quiet. The drinks came in large glasses. They were more like doubles or triples. Doug smiled approvingly.

"This is my kind of place," he said. He finished his Stoli before I lifted my glass.

"Remember when you said no more hard liquor?"

"Yeah," he said.

"Maybe we shouldn't drink this week."

"I used to drink to feel good. Now I drink so I don't feel bad. I don't know if I could stop."

"So let's not stop, just cut down a little."

"When we get back to the City, we'll cut down. The wines are better there."

"What difference does that make?" I asked.

"When the wine is good, you don't need as much."

"Oh," I said.

The waitress brought our food and another drink for each of us.

We drank our drinks. We had some more.

Before we knew it, the waitress came and told us the bar was closing for a private party. She smiled and asked where we were going. Doug pulled out the envelope and showed her the address.

Joey came by our table. "Maybe I'd better drive you there. It's not far. You can keep the rental car here and pick it up after fishing tomorrow."

"Thank you. That'll work. We don't have a rental car."

That seemed hilarious to me.

The waitress said thanks, have a nice night, or something like that.

Joey took us to his car and drove us to the condo. The place was a straight shot on Old Montauk Highway, on the Atlantic Ocean, with the bay and a lake not far away. It was in a condo complex, with an exercise area and a Club House.

We exited the car. A police vehicle passed us. Joey gave it a wave.

We were quickly inside. Brochures covered the table in the entryway. The condo was for sale, asking price $4.2 million dollars.

The place was large: fifty-five hundred square feet. It reminded me of every Ritz Carlton I'd ever been in, except for the Atlantic Ocean right in front of us, which admittedly added something. The living room had a gigantic flat screen TV over the fireplace and floor-to-ceiling windows facing the ocean, truly a million dollar view.

Doug turned a chair around, so he could face the ocean. "Say, Pete, think you could scare up some drinks?"

I found a refrigerator that contained plenty of ice and sliced lemons and limes. I saw about eight different kinds of vodka in the freezer and chose a Ravenscroft Crystal lead-free decanter filled with Crystal.

I opened a cupboard next to the refrigerator. Rye whiskies, the finest scotches, an array of wines of all vintages, arranged by countries of origin and separated into parts of the countries: France, Italy, Australia, and the United States.

A note tacked to the cupboard said, "There's a wine cellar in the basement. Enjoy!" I took the note and crumpled it, stuffing it in my pocket. It would be too much for Doug and me. We'd be obligated to accept the challenge and drink it all. It's been my experience that when I fight my demons, I always lose. Better to surrender gracefully.

It reminded me of an old story, which I thought Doug would enjoy.

"Dougie, do you know the one about the man who got locked in a basement and tried to escape?"

"No, I don't think so."

"Well, there's this guy locked in a basement. He sees a door and walks outside. A gorilla hits him once or twice. The guy runs back into the basement. A little while later, the man walks outside again, and this time the gorilla really lets him have it. So the man goes back inside.

"Here's the thing. The guy comes out again and no gorilla. So the dumb son of a bitch goes looking for the gorilla."

"A metaphor for the drinking life?" Doug asked.

"No, my autobiography," I replied.

"On that note, I need a drink," Doug said.

"How about vodka?" I said.

"With ice and lime, if available."

I filled the ice bucket and put it, the decanter, and the two drinks on a tray.

Doug was reading a brochure. He looked up and saw the decanter.

He laughed. "My, my, this is the life. You do know that after three drinks all vodkas taste the same?"

"I'm sure you're right but this bottle is prettier."

"Scenic, like the view," Doug said. "This Condo costs over one thousand dollars a square foot. Might as well enjoy it."

"Agreed." I said.

"Do you know what the most expensive real estate in the world is?"

"Not a clue."

"Think of your friend Dylan. I've been trying to get this line into a book but it never quite fit."

I sat down, stared at the ocean, and sipped at my drink. This stuff was dynamite. It was smooth going down. It probably was 120 proof, if there were such a thing.

"Yeah," he said. "Dylan's vagina, the most expensive piece of real estate in the world."

"That's a cynical way of looking at things," I said.

"Yes, it is," Doug said. "I insist that any woman with sense knows she can't believe anything a man says, unless she's ugly. Then she can get the truth from a man but she wouldn't want it."

I groaned.

We walked outside onto the beach. The sand was white and clean. It was high tide, the waves crashing into the shore. A lone surfer struggled with the six-foot waves. Anglers were packing up their gear. The moon was a crescent-shaped whisper in the sky. A few adults were cooking hot dogs over a raging fire, flames shooting upwards into the sky while children played football in the sand nearby.

We walked along the beach, breathing in the sea air, hearing the surf pounding against the shore. Clouds draped over the moon. There's no softer light than moonlight. We felt the beach, unseasonably warm, sandy, and dark. The lights from the motels and houses along the beach winked at us. New Orleans street funk streamed out of one of the houses as Trombone Shorty's *Do to Me* filled the air.

We ended up at an outdoor café. An SUV with big wheels sped down the street, blasting Biggie Small so loud that the vehicle was heaving with sound. The waiter at the café shook his head in contrapuntal melody. It reminded me of the Ferrari in Paris—different music, different car, but vital and alive.

"Like a moth to a flame," Doug said. "That's us, Petey, moths to a flame. Let's get some drinks."

"Why not go back to the condo? Better booze."

"No offense, Petey. The best booze is drunk with others. Let's not deprive the town of the honor of my company."

A few people were finishing dinner. The bar inside was jumping. A lot of people and loud music, cigarette smoke snaking through the room. I saw Bernie but tried to avoid him.

Siegel shouted, "Peter, it's me."

We stopped, unable to ignore him at such close range.

"Hey Peter, how have you been?"

"Good," I said.

"Good trip out here? I took a helicopter. The Long Island Rail Road isn't very scenic."

"Bernie, you remember Doug?"

"Of course. We were just together at the fights. How are you, Doug?" Siegel asked. "Where are you two staying?"

"A little condo down the street," I told him.

The three of us walked into the back of the bar. We were the oldest people there. I didn't recognize any of the music. No one looked at us.

Doug ignored Siegel. We ordered drinks. Doug asked for any kind of bourbon on the rocks. After three or four drinks, Doug said, "That's it for me, Pete. Let's head back."

"Where are we going tomorrow?" Bernie asked.

"Surf fishing. We've made the arrangements. We get lunch and the best fishing in the area. We'll pick you up at 7:15. Why not bring some wine and a few glasses? That can be your contribution," I said.

Bernie agreed. He left without comment, a first.

Doug and I walked back in silence. When we got inside, Doug poured himself a large glass of the Crystal but didn't bother with ice or fruit. He grabbed an unopened bottle of vodka and went to his room.

I tried to turn on the big TV, which was connected to a cable box and a sound system. I never got all three on at the same time. I went over to the window and stared out at the darkness. Flipping the light switch illuminated the terrace. The sea was calm now, the waves receding.

I liked staring out into the emptiness. I knew that the ocean was alive and moving, even when seemingly still. I felt as though I were looking at something meaningful, but I didn't know what it was.

I cracked open one of the side windows. A rush of warm sea air filled the large room. Then all was still. I fell asleep in the chair.

I heard sounds in the middle of the night, a bird on the roof, a siren far off in the distance. Then the ocean woke up. Thunder roared. Lightning lit up the sky, the surf, and the water. I rushed to make sure no water had seeped in through the open window and shut it.

Walking to my bedroom, I heard Doug muttering in his sleep. Alcohol puts you to sleep but not always calmly.

I slept dead to the world and to the alarm.

Chapter 13

Doug banged on my door. "Time to get up, Sleeping Beauty. The fish are waiting. "

"I'm going to take a quick shower," I told him. I loved the enormous steam shower, water pounded hot and heavy from jets attacking from every position, washing off the dust of the road and the worry from my soul.

Doug had been busy. He'd brewed coffee. He put a carton of milk and some sugar on the table, with two big mugs, filling a thermos for later. Doug had even placed the fishing gear in the front hallway.

A discreet knock at exactly 7:00 AM revealed Joey, our reliable eighteen year old, wearing well-ironed shorts, a t-shirt, and a light windbreaker. Even his sneakers were spotless. His hat had flies attached to it.

We got into Joey's car. Joey drove quickly and smoothly, with no wasted movements. His Jeep was as immaculate as his person, with not a tinge of fish odor or a scrap of dust. The car was old, but the engine purred and the chrome glistened.

Joey motioned to a large bag in the back. "We'll eat when we get to the fishing site."

"No problem. A friend of ours is coming along. Is that okay?

"Sure," Joey said.

I told him the name of the hotel and added, "He's not really a friend, just someone we know who wants to tag along."

Joey made a quick right turn and drove to Siegel's hotel. Siegel was standing outside and came over to the car.

"I'm sorry. I'll be ready in fifteen minutes."

"Your friend," said Doug, looking annoyed.

Joey parked the car. "I'll be back in a little bit," he said, and left.

Doug and I walked to the café we'd been to the day before and ordered coffee.

"Possible to get a shot of something in this?" Doug asked. The waiter said he'd arrange it. Doug stuffed some bills on the table. We had our Irish coffee.

The town looked fresh in its early morning innocence. I enjoyed sitting in the cafe sipping my coffee. The salty sea air enveloped us, making promises of a good day.

Gulls swooped down, vacuuming the remains left behind by the street cleaner. The motels were pristine, with their fresh white paint and large, clean windows. An employee from one of the motels was washing its windows, using an outsized brush. The waiter brought us more coffee with whiskey, this time with fresh whipped cream on top.

We basked in the morning sun and savored the sweetness of the coffee braced by the whiskey. I would have been happy sitting there all day, watching the people, feeling the breeze, and drinking my coffee. We could see Siegel's hotel. I could care less when he came down.

"I'm surprised they let him in," Doug said. "This whole town has been sanitized."

Doug was right. This was a clean town, ready to greet tourists but circumspect in its judgment.

The phone rang—Dr. Turk. I remembered I was still waiting for test results. He was calling pretty early, probably before he started surgery. I decided not to answer. If it were bad news it would keep. I didn't want to ruin my fishing.

I clicked the mode to voice mail. He called right back. Not a good sign, I thought. I didn't want to hear what he had to say. I had a bad feeling.

I came back to the table. After we each had another coffee, Siegel walked out of his hotel. He had on dark shades and looked a little unsteady on his feet.

He stood quietly for a moment. He wore a light shirt and shorts and clean sneakers, an older, heavier, bigger-muscled Joey.

Joey, Doug and I got in the car.

"He's a writer, too," I told Joey. "Not like Doug, of course, but he's a good writer."

Joe made a U-turn and stopped in front of Bernie. He got out of the car, walked up to Siegel and shook his hand, opening the back door for him.

Siegel carried a large bag of food, trying to be a grateful guest. It would have been better if he'd been ready on time, I thought.

Joey drove quickly through town. I saw more motels and more Atlantic Ocean, large oceanfront homes with vast decks and landscaped patios, expensive-looking furniture and hot tubs. It was a strange mixture of sterile real estate and powerful ocean.

We passed a few people, some on bicycles, some walking, and a handful jogging. No one was speaking, singing, or making noise. It was like an eerie foreign film, except for the strip malls. We drove further into green areas with tall trees, up a hill and down the other side.

I saw some very old houses and little cottages, a town with a shabby garage and a rickety greasy spoon of a diner. We drove down a hill and out of the tall trees. The sight of the ocean hit us like a machine gun. There were wide expanses of sand and ocean. A few fishermen stood in the sand, casting into the water.

Joey pulled up away from them, parking his car on the sand. He got out and starting unloading the car. Doug and I helped him move the gear to the sand, placing it on the waterproof blanket Joey had laid out. Joey set up a beach umbrella, chairs, and a little table, digging a hole deep enough to insert the coolers underneath.

Siegel stepped out of the car, holding our breakfast. We ate quickly.

Joey walked over to the three anglers and talked to them. They shook their heads no. He glanced at the cooler they had filled with fish. He smiled at them and shook his head. He walked back to us.

Siegel asked Joe if there were fish here.

"There are always fish. It's just that they don't always bite. Have you ever surf fished before, Bernie?"

"Fished out of a fishing boat a few times. Didn't like it much. I like things with a little more action," he said.

Joey laughed. Doug and I smiled.

A beautiful young girl wearing blue jeans, a flannel shirt, and a New York Yankee baseball cap sauntered by with a little wiggle in her walk. She had a rod and reel in one hand, and a cooler tucked under her other arm. She looked right through us. She walked to her red pick-up parked in the sand, putting the cooler on the truck.

She got into the pick-up and magically pulled out a Heineken. She turned the car on. Springsteen's *Spirit in the Night* blasted out through the speakers. The girl mouthed the words as she drove away. Her left rear tire hit a big puddle in the sand , pouring water over us. We saw her in her side view mirror laughing as she sped off.

"No one speak," said Doug. "We've just seen God."

I took out a pack of cigarettes, and offered them around. Joe shook his head. Siegel looked disgusted.

"I thought you quit."

"I did. Fight night did me in."

Doug pulled out a cigar and lit up. "Ah, the despoilment of nature," said Doug.

We got our rods out, heeding Joe's directions. Siegel listened intently.

"It's not as easy as you think," Doug said. "They swim away. They'll give you a hell of a fight before they do."

Joey inspected our rods and said they were fine. He had bloodworms, squid, shrimp, and mullet in one of the coolers he'd buried in the sand, as well as a couple of hook-bottom and fireball rigs.

"I was hoping to get some blues, but we're a little late. The fireballs will help. I have a few lures here as well. Blues and striped bass love them."

He handed us some sand spikes—pieces of pipe to be shoved into the sand. That way we wouldn't ruin rods or reels.

"Sand loves reels, like nails to a magnet. Sand wrecks your reels in a second," he said. "I'm going to show you the best way to cast. Don't get discouraged. I've been surf fishing since I was three."

He showed us the motion and cast a few times with an empty hook. The line went out sure and steady, about a hundred yards farther than the angler down the beach had managed.

Siegel mimicked Joe's movement without a rod, staring at his fingers on the reel.

I managed to get the line into the water a few yards from where we stood. Doug did better because he'd surf-fished all over the world. Joey was a young, good-natured kid who was fishing more because he enjoyed it than because he was getting paid.

Siegel's first cast was a disaster, as was his second and third. Then he got it. His line sailed out, long and true.

Siegel got the first bite. He fought doggedly and landed the fish. The first led to the second, the second to the third, and the third to many more. We enjoyed the rush as we landed fish after fish.

"Who was that sexy reporter from ESPN that we ate with in Pamplona?" Doug asked.

"Erin," I said. "You were really smitten with her."

"She was a good girl. She could handle her scotch," Doug said.

We stopped for lunch. Doug had brought some red wine that he'd buried in the sand. It was a perfect temperature. Doug and I drank the wine.

"A toast to brevity," I said.

"You are a gentleman and a scholar," Doug said.

"And terse as well," Siegel said.

"How many good things I could say about brevity," Doug said.

"Yes, but you won't. It's no accident that the Gettysburg address was short," I said, quoting my favorite author.

Joey and Siegel enjoyed the food and walked off to view the idyllic setting.

Doug dozed off. I decided to check my messages. Turk's voice came through, calm and reassuring. "Nothing important. Give me a call when you have a chance. No worries but I need to talk to you."

I thought of calling him but decided against it. I closed my eyes. Joe and Bernie returned to find us sleeping.

"That's it for fishing, gentlemen. The fish have stopped biting," Joe said. "I've cleaned your fish and will bring them to your condo. Mr. Siegel can bring his to the motel. The café will cook it for him."

He began cleaning up. Siegel helped him pack and load the car. Doug and I slept on the way back. Joey unloaded the car and offered to give us the fish.

"No," I said. "You keep them. I think we'll do some sight-seeing tomorrow. The rest of our friends are coming. Even if they don't, can you take us fly fishing the following day?"

"Consider it done."

I paid him. Doug gave Joey a tip, which must have been generous, since he said thank you about four times. We told Siegel we'd meet him at nine for dinner.

The jeep drove off.

The condo was ice cold, which was perfect. I jumped in the shower while Doug turned on the TV in the living room. I toweled myself off, fell on my bed and was out.

When I got up, Doug was nursing a scotch, staring out at the ocean. I poured myself some Elit Vodka, which I thought was a cousin of Stoli, but much better, smoother, a bigger kick.

I sat down next to Doug, facing the water.

"This would be the place to write a novel," I said.

"Why don't you?" he asked.

"A good question. One I've asked myself many times. Still don't have an answer. Want to walk into town?"

"Sure, what's a mile between friends?"

I didn't think it was even half a mile. We walked along the side of the road, one foot in front of the other.

We had built up a sweat and a thirst by the time we got into town. Siegel was at a table for four, drinking a soft drink. He had guacamole and chips in front of him and sat motionless, staring into the street.

He didn't know if we knew about him and Dylan. That made him more insufferable than usual. He didn't get that many people had taken trips with Dylan, and that it meant less than nothing.

We sat at his table. Our waitress came right over.

"Joseph brought your fish here and the cook fried it up— really good," she said. "Do you want an appetizer?"

"Sure. Why don't you surprise us?" Doug said. "We're expecting a few more friends."

"They won't be here," Siegel said.

"Why not?" asked Doug. "They said they'd be here."

"They're very unreliable," I said. "The only thing you can count on is that you can't count on them."

"I don't think they'll come," Siegel said, speaking as though he knew something which we were unable to appreciate. That kind of condescension was always annoying, but particularly so from Siegel, a man who was here on sufferance.

Doug was irritated. "I'll bet they'll come," he said.

"There's no way they're coming. I know her much better than you, Doug. Tell him, Petey," Siegel said.

"My good man, you may know her better than I, but it's a safe assumption she's found someone better than you," Doug said.

"Enough, guys. They'll come, unless they don't, and if they do, they'll be a lot later than you expect. That's the way they are. That's something I would bet on," I said.

"Bet on a sure thing? There's no fun in that." Doug beckoned to the waitress. "Let's have some sangría."

After a short while, the waitress put the pitcher of sangría on the table. She returned with a vast array of appetizers. Fresh fried calamari, cooked minutes before, light and tasty; shrimp in a garlic butter sauce with parsley that melted in your mouth, and mozzarella sticks fresh cooked with a delicate tomato and basil sauce.

The salad dressing, fresh-made orange poppy seed with the taste of real oranges, covered a salad with different kinds of lettuce, peppers, tomatoes, and onions. The place was giving us our money's worth.

The waitress brought us another pitcher of the sangría.

"This is made with peach brandy. It's really strong," she said.

"Have some, my darling," Doug said.

"Thank you," she said.

We drank a lot and ate a little fish. Bernie was very quiet, almost morose. He got up abruptly, nodded at us, and left.

We called the waitress over to settle up. "Mr. Siegel took care of it, and the tip, too," she said. "He even tipped the cook. Is there anything else I can get you?"

"No, thanks," Doug said.

She smiled as she walked away.

"Do you think they'll get here tonight?" Doug asked.

"I've never known either one of them to be on time," I said.

"It's too bad Siegel doesn't share that trait. He's your friend. I guess he's all right, but there's something off about him—like slightly spoiled milk," Doug said.

I saw Siegel walking toward us.

"The guy can't stand missing anything. Here he comes again," I said.

On cue, Siegel sat down.

"Doug, do you think you changed as you've gotten older," I asked.

"You get to be a certain age, and it's not very old, maybe forty or so, and you realize you've lost your innocence," said Doug. "You wouldn't cross the street to save someone's life, well, I wouldn't. You actually have. When good things happen, you should grab on to them because they'll never last. If you have a life with little tragedy, make sure you're grateful because you're just damned lucky."

He drank more of his drink.

"It's hard to keep going," he muttered.

I put my hand on top of his.

"No, my friend, you can't give up," I said. "I can't compre-
hend the pain you feel. I only hope you have a moment of
peace someday, or even more—happiness."

"I don't know any good writers who are happy," Bernie
said.

"You know the real trouble with being a writer?" Doug
asked.

"Great writers are great listeners. The problem is when
you listen, you hear things—and a lot of it is drivel."

"Oh," Siegel said. "Are you talking about me?"

"No, I'm talking about me. I wake up in the morning and
think the world's coming to an end. It's an effort to get up, to
brush my teeth, to get dressed. That's why you're so amazing,
Petey. You just keep going," Doug said, lines of grief etched in
his face, making him look a thousand years old.

"I'll drink to that," Bernie said.

"No more drinking for me tonight," said Doug, "We're
going to head back to the condo."

"No problem," Siegel said. He got up and left, again without
another word. We left the restaurant and walked toward the
condo. I saw a church in the town with the lights on.

"I'd go inside," I said, "but it's probably an AA meeting."

"It might be people importuning their God," Doug said.
"I'm going back to the condo."

"Go ahead. I'm going to go inside."

I walked into the church, a modest building. I foraged
around until I found the nave and chapel. I sat in a pew,
thinking that I wanted to get up because it was absurd. I
couldn't believe I was wasting my time. I had often wished I
was a true believer. I wasn't, and I couldn't start now.

I wished I believed I had a purpose in life. I wished I
experienced the joy of the presence of a Supreme Being. I
wanted a spiritual awakening. I had long since learned that
wanting something doesn't make it happen. It seemed to
me Catholicism was a great religion. It was too bad so many
priests were Catholic.

My near-death experience had left me no closer to God;
it left me numb. I wanted a white light experience but there

was no light, nothing to guide my way. I was alive and very sick and would die soon, and it would be as though I had never been. I would sink quietly in the nothingness from whence I came.

I walked outside. My cheeks were damp because I was crying. It was late. It was dark, with no moon in the sky. I shivered in the cold ocean air as I plodded back to the condo.

Doug was in his room. I asked him what he would say if he met the God he'd rejected.

"What would I say to God? I'd get him a cold beer. I'd find him a beautiful whore and I'd say 'I'm goddamned sorry for not believing in You.'"

He walked out of his room.

I went to the bar and poured myself some wonderfully expensive vodka. I stared at the ocean from the living room window, sitting in the overstuffed chair with my feet up on the coffee table, drinking from my glass, and thinking how nice it would be if prayers were answered.

Somewhere, sometime, someone had told me Jews didn't make prayers of supplication, only prayers of gratitude. I wondered if they prayed in La Vernet or Dachau. What could they find to pray about if they didn't ask for help in getting out? They weren't thanking God for putting them there, I'm sure of that.

I checked my cell phone and the landline in the condo. No one had called. I sat for a long time, drinking vodka and looking at the ocean. The waves rolled in. The waves rolled out. Soft murmuring sounds promised a beautiful calm day and good fishing.

In the distance, a radio played. I heard the whisper of a lyrical melody that spoke to me, telling me it was part of something bigger, grander, better. The peace I felt made me think of God. My grandmother, a pious Presbyterian, told me all prayers were answered, but that the answer wasn't necessarily yes.

My cell phone rang. I jumped up from my chair. I'd forgotten where I put the phone. The phone stopped ringing and started again. I rummaged around. The phone had slipped under the cushion in the chair. I saw it was Bernie and almost didn't answer.

"They didn't catch the train. I'm going back to the motel."

"Did they call?"

"Not me, or I wouldn't be here at the train station."

"Didn't call us either."

"I knew they weren't coming," Bernie said,

"I can't say I'm surprised," I said.

Siegel hung up without saying goodbye.

Doug came out of his room eating an apple. "So they didn't come?"

"Nope."

Doug's blackberry played music that signified a text.

He looked at the message. "'Took a trip to Atlantic City, be there henceforth' Whatever that means.'

"It means they won't be here tomorrow," I said.

"So let's enjoy our time without them," Doug said.

"Let's go to bed and get some good fishing in tomorrow. I'd love to leave Siegel behind," I said.

"Why do we hate him so much?" I asked.

"Hate is too strong a word. Despise, loathe, feel contempt for, but not hate. He's not good enough to reward with my hate. Let's have another drink and call it a night."

We had a few more drinks and looked at the ocean.

"Did you know that he was with Dylan?" Doug asked me.

"Yes, I heard that."

"He also said he's meeting Dylan in Palm Beach for the polo matches."

"She'll be done with him by then," I said, getting annoyed.

"Don't get angry. What's the point? We fish, drink wine, have some laughs. How did you happen to ask this guy to come fishing with us anyway?"

"Siegel invited himself."

Doug took a healthy swig of his drink. He stared out at the ocean.

"Isn't he the guy you sent to California with a letter asking me to take him around? I was out on that terrible movie in

LA. Say, not meeting Siegel was the only good thing about the picture."

He finished his drink and got up to pour another one.

"There's something very, very off about him."

"Agreed."

"Let's dump Siegel. He gives me the creeps, and it takes a lot to do that."

"Okay," I said. "Goodnight."

We each went into our bedroom, he to sleep and perchance to dream, me to toss and turn until I walked back into the living room and fell asleep to the Atlantic Ocean serenade.

Chapter 14

I got up at 5:30 and showered and shaved. I poured myself some orange juice. I thought about adding vodka but kept it to orange juice.

Doug wasn't up yet. I walked out onto the terrace. My cell phone rang. It was Siegel. "I'm at the airport. There's no way they're showing up. They're partying late every night and have no interest in us. Dylan went to sleep early when we were together," he said.

I thought she must have been bored out of her mind.

"Take care, Bernie," I said and hung up.

Doug came outside, hair wet from his shower, drinking coffee. He had a cup for me as well. A young boy about four, walked past the condo with his mother. Doug avoided looking at him.

"Cute kid," I said, absentmindedly.

Doug didn't answer.

He had lost a child. Tragedy never leaves you. His five-year-old son had climbed over the railing in the rotunda of the Ritz Carlton in Palm Beach.

"He fell from the sky. He was there, and then he wasn't there anymore," Doug had told me on a drunken night years earlier.

Everything after that was a single event followed by another event meaning nothing. That's when real life superimposed itself on his idyllic existence. The fabric of his soul ripped that night. On that night he became a great writer.

Doug had said, "People tell you that time heals all wounds and that you forget. I wish it did. It doesn't. He's the first thing I think of every morning and the last thing I dream of before I wake up."

Doug and his wife, the best of all his wives, divorced within the year. You would have thought the boy's death would have shocked him sober but it hadn't. Doug kept on writing and drinking. Nothing changed, except for the omnipresence of the shadow of death that never left him.

I looked at him. He looked at me, as though regretting telling me of his son. He could have forgotten that he'd told me. You can't tell with drinkers, I thought.

We went inside and drank more coffee.

My phone rang. It was Turk.

I got up and walked away, my feet cold on the tile. I felt myself trembling.

"How's it going?" Turk asked.

"Give it to me. I know you've got bad news," I said.

"Not really. Your liver enzymes are slightly elevated. I believe it's not related to the lymphoma. You'd better cut down on your alcohol consumption. We need to keep a careful watch though. We're waiting for the rest of the results. Do you have a cough?"

"No."

"Night sweats?"

"No."

"Are you bruising easily?"

"No. Why are you asking me this? I thought you said it was nothing."

"I'm sure it's nothing, just being careful. You're fine. I'll call you in a few days to check on you."

"Why so much attention to a healthy patient?"

"All right. I won't call in a few days. Is that better?"

"Thanks, Doc."

I walked back to Doug, hopeful that Turk was telling the truth.

"Is there anything worth seeing or doing other than fishing?" Doug asked.

"Do you want to see something magnificent?"

"What's that?"

"Winter surfing."

"Sounds like a plan," Doug said.

We called a car to take us to one of the surfing beaches. I grabbed my gear and a cooler filled with assorted beverages. Fifteen minutes later we were at the beach. I told the cabbie to pick us up in two hours.

Normally, winter surfing meant hours of shoveling driveways and de-icing cars. You parked at ten o'clock in the morning and came back four hours later, and yours would be the only footprints in the snow. Today was more like a spring day, but the water was deadly cold. Winter transformed dazzling sunlight and warm water into icy darkness. It wasn't safe, but it was glorious.

Doug and I sat on two beach chairs propped in the sand. We watched the surfers on the lonely beach for a long while.

A guy wearing Ray bans, with long blond hair and a muscular build limped over to us. He had a cast on his left leg and wore a halo collar.

I smiled at him and beckoned to an empty chair. He eased himself into the seat.

"Buy you a drink?" I asked.

"Thanks mate, but with the painkillers I'm on, I'd try to ride a wave."

"Coca Cola?"

"Great."

I pulled a coke out of the cooler and a Corona for myself. We clicked bottles.

Doug heard the sound, opened his eyes, and reached for a drink. He looked at the guy, a surfer who had battled the waves and lost.

"Hi," he said. "Doug Gosling."

"The writer?"

"Yeah," he said.

"Automobile accident," the blond guy said.

"Really?" I asked.

"No. I'm a little sick of people asking me why I keep surfing when I keep getting hurt."

"You must be good," Doug said.

"Is that sarcastic?"

"No," Doug said. "If you were terrible, nobody would care. It was more an observation than a question."

"Well, here's a question for you. Why do you think I do it?"

Doug said, "You're looking for the timeless transcendence of ordinary life. You've experienced the profane and are looking for the sacred, and it's here."

The blond guy and I stared at him.

"Only in extreme circumstances, where death is a constant companion, can you attain sacred moments. It is real and it is authentic. And when you participate in the experience, you are authentic too."

"Whatever, dude," the kid said. He raised his glass to Doug, took a drink, got up, and walked away.

"What was that all about?" I asked.

"Hey, pay due deference to my insincerity, please."

I shrugged.

"Hemingway thought the key to writing was pity and irony. Bernie's pitiful and you're ironic. Perhaps the two of you should make a buddy movie."

Doug took a swig of his Bloody Mary and a gulp of his coffee.

"I'm not sure irony is necessary, but you do need empathy or else you can't understand someone, and without understanding I doubt you'd write anything worthwhile," I told him.

"Thank you, William Shakespeare. It's a good thing you make your living taking pictures."

Doug laughed. "Don't you get it? I'm a writer. That means I lie. So I lie in life as well. Got to keep my hand in."

"It's good to know the truth. That way you know when you're lying," I said.

"Actually, I don't fool anyone but myself, and that's the only person I have to fool," Doug said.

Doug finished off his Bloody Mary. We were alone on the beach watching the surf and the surfers.

"Have some more coffee," I said. "It'll wake you up."

"Don't you mean sober me up? Why would I want that? My biggest regrets are the moments I'm sober. You know what your trouble is? Remember when you were always writing that blog. Even if they made a book from it, it would still be the first draft of a not very good novel. With all the millions of words from all the millions of blogs, nothing worthwhile has ever been published." Doug drank a little coffee and stared into his cup.

"The trouble with the Internet is that it's not real. You've lost touch with the world, and you don't understand the power of the unuttered thought. I see you drinking and talking, talking and drinking, and retreating to typing on a keyboard, saying nothing."

"Sounds like a great life," I told him, ironically. "Do I do anything worthwhile?"

"Your pictures are beautiful, raw and honest. Your blog was worthless. I've also heard you're impotent."

"Ah, now you're getting personal. If you want to know, I had a fight with cancer years ago, and it left me with scars. What's your excuse?"

"Ah, don't go there. Certain things shouldn't be discussed. Something women don't understand. Everything doesn't have to be said."

"Ah, the power of the unuttered word."

"Are you okay now?"

"I've been cancer-free for five years—an important milestone. I'd appreciate it if we never mention it again."

"Forgotten already. Let's have another drink."

"I think I've had enough."

"Are you casting aspersions on my drinking?" Doug asked, laughing.

"No. No. Not at all. Interesting for a writer, though, not everything has to be said."

"A writer learns that early on. You can't fall in love with your own words, because you have to cut at least half of them. The intelligent, best read, and least talented writers get it, but that's because their words aren't worth keeping."

I didn't say anything.

"Mind if I change the subject? You're my favorite person on earth that doesn't have a vagina."

"Doug, at the cost of being a cliché, may I quote you again? Not everything has to be said, especially that."

Doug smiled and asked, "Notwithstanding the above, do you want to hear more?"

"Not really," I said. "Let's enjoy the silence."

We sat on the beach for awhile, watching the surfers.

Doug said, "I've studied these guys. Do you know Greg Noll? He said that when he got older, later, much later, he realized he was always on the edge, on a death wish wave. When you're doing it, you're a king. When you stop, you miss it, like cocaine or heroin. Without it you're nothing."

"Fitzgerald said that there was something awe-inspiring in one who has lost all inhibitions," I replied.

We watched a surfer take a big wave.

It was dark and cold. The white of the wave was a border between earth and sky. The surf was loud. The surfer turned in, and that was it. The ocean swallowed him.

Everyone swam toward him. They lifted him onto his board while someone else grabbed the other board, which was spinning around and around looking for another victim.

They brought him to the sand. He was fine, but the surfers seemed subdued.

"Is there a metaphysical connection there? Is that what they're looking for, God? Are they looking for God?" Doug asked.

"Or death, or pain, or a way to while away the hours?" I said.

"Maybe they're just idiots," Doug said.

"Time for a small snack, more wine, and a nap. Maybe the lovebirds will be here. We'll have a rip-roaring night. Actually I could do without Dodo. His hospitality is becoming..."

"Burdensome?"

"Onerous. We do well with our gallon jugs of Gallo. You don't mind if you spill it, and the bottles have a certain pedestrian charm."

"And after the third drink, it all tastes the same," I laughed.

The cab was waiting for us. We went back to the condo. Doug went into his room.

I was restless. This was my favorite time of the day. I decided to go for a stroll on the beach. I grabbed my camera, hoping to catch the sun setting over the water.

I called out to Doug, "I'm going for a walk. I'll be back in an hour."

Doug didn't answer.

"Doug, you heard me, right?"

He didn't say anything so I went into his room. He just got up and left. His eyes were red. He'd been reading *Sodom and Gomorrah Play Vaudeville*, his Pulitzer Prize winning novel.

I picked up the book and saw the Dedication. I read it for the hundredth time.

To My Son

> *The worst words a man can say are 'I lost my child today.' I see your smile. I hear your laughter. I feel your tiny hand in mine. They put a white sheet over your face. I can't believe you are gone.*
>
> *I thought I gave you life. The reality is that you gave me a life. I pray you felt loved. I did not love until loving you. You were born and the world was good. Then, in an instant, it was over. I can't believe you are gone.*
>
> *It is the living who suffer and the living who die, daily, in their despair.*
>
> *They say that thousands of young children etched out butterflies with their fingers to symbolize their refusal to die when they were thrust into the ovens. Yes, thrust into the ovens by sadistic ghouls who had not a scintilla of doubt or guilt. I should have cried for them.*
>
> *But I am like everyone else. My tragedy is my own and your death is the worst imaginable. I died with you, and die again each day. I hope there is a heaven. I know there is a hell.*

I wish to forget but I cannot. I hate myself for wanting to forget. I spend my days longing to die so that I can hold your hand in heaven.
I cherished you then and I cherish you now. My book is dedicated to you, my son. I love you.

Doug was one hell of a writer. Every time I read this, no matter what outrageous thing he had done or said, he became my friend again.

I started walking. I heard panting and footsteps behind me. Doug fell into step with me. We enjoyed a companionable silence.

"I am so sorry, Doug. I am just so sorry."

Doug didn't say anything but trudged along. We walked a long way without saying a word.

"I'm going to sit at the café, and start writing my blog."

"The symbolic trash can?" he asked.

"Has anybody written one page that has the wisdom of Plato or Aristotle? Maybe too much information is bad. We can't assimilate it, let alone synthesize it," I said.

"Maybe the real problem is that we're not Plato or Aristotle."

We kept on, each in our private little realm, on a downward spiral, one more blip on life's path. We ambled past the café, and reversed ourselves, going to 'our' seats.

Chapter 15

The waitress came right over and smiled. "What'll it be, gentlemen?"

"How about a beer?"

"Sure. We have Michelob on tap."

"Sounds delightful," Doug said.

"Thanks for the fish. We all had a feast tonight," she said.

Joey had been spreading our largesse.

"I wonder if our friends have arrived. They'd find this place in a New York minute."

"Lots of people came in," the waitress said. "What do they look like?"

"If you have to ask, they haven't come," I said.

"They'll come when they come and if they don't, we'll see if there's some trout fishing nearby," Doug replied.

He smiled.

The waitress came back a few minutes later with the beers. She went to a nearby table and took their order.

"I guess we should call our friend Joe," I said.

"Let's call him later. Let's sit here and rejoice in our blessings. Let us rejoice and give thanks."

"You forgot believe."

"I do believe. I believe in much. I rejoice in little because of what I believe in."

"I've forgotten what I believe in, but I still believe in it," I said.

"How could we be drunk on one beer?"

Three women walked over to our table. They were in their early forties, a good age for women, disillusioned enough to be realistic but still with some hope left. They were all attractive. One was a little overweight, the other two fantastically well-built. Doug said, "Welcome, young ladies. Please sit down."

The women looked at each and moved to sit down. I brought a chair over and the plump brunette with soft eyes sat in it.

"Thanks," she said.

"My pleasure," I said.

"Aren't you...?" the prettiest one in the group, the one with the shortest skirt and the tightest tee, asked Doug.

She would look like a dishrag beside Dylan.

Where was she, my darling Dylan, and who was she bedeviling?

"Someday I'll go someplace and a woman will sit down next to me and say hi. And she won't ask me who I am, and I'll marry her," Doug interrupted, with a pleasant smile.

The chubby woman got up and said, "If she didn't know who you were, I doubt she'd sit down with you."

She walked away. The other two women waited a moment and walked after her. I guess they knew about nasty drunks.

"Ah, I've run off our companions. I would have liked your lady of the night far better. I hate amateurs. So back to prayer. Should we kneel?"

The waitress had brought us two more beers, which we drank to prayers and kneeling.

We did not kneel and we did not pray.

"You think being Catholic is what crippled us? Or maybe having Catholic mothers?"

"I'm not Catholic."

"Could have fooled me."

"So what crippled Siegel?"

"I resent that," Doug said. "I may be crippled but I'm not a quadriplegic. That guy is doomed."

"He's not here, Doug. Let's not raise his ghost."

"You're right about that."

The waitress came over and said, "We've got some new wines in. Australian. Supposed to be good."

"Do you sample the wines?"

"I don't drink," she said. "But don't let it stop you. I don't like the taste of alcohol."

We laughed. "You don't drink alcohol for the taste. Bring us a bottle of that tasty wine," I said.

The waitress came back with the wine and an ice bucket.

"Is this white wine?" I asked. "I'm sorry. This is a month with an r in it. We drink red wine."

"No problem. I'll get you something good," the girl who didn't drink because she didn't like the taste of it, said.

"The next drink is always inevitable," Doug said.

"Nothing is inevitable," said the waitress.

"We shall meet again. I shall be older and no wiser. That's inevitable," Doug said.

"Doug, you're drunk," I said.

"On two beers?"

"Sure."

"It's the heat of this early spring evening."

"Seems cold to me." I was cold, wearing a light sweater that was no protection against the frosty winds whipping around the café.

"Do you know what you are, my good friend. You're the world's greatest photographer."

"And you, sir, are the world's greatest writer."

The waitress walked over to the table. "And you, madam, are the world's greatest waitress," I said.

"Unfortunately, that's a transient title, belonging to the beautiful savior pouring the next drink," said Doug. "I once had a dream that all the waitresses who served me, intervened me in the nude, and put me in a rehab unit in a hospital. I insisted I belonged on a psych ward."

"How did that work out?" I asked

"Loved the drugs, hated the patients."

"That's some dream," I said.

We went inside, the plump lady smiling at me, her two friends glaring. They had picked up two locals, and we knew which lady was going home alone.

"I am tired," Doug said.

"Me too."

"Think they'd let us sleep at this table?"

"You know what? I think it's time for us to leave," I said, and settled up with the waitress.

"Okay. If your friends come, I'll point them in your direction."

We folded ourselves into a taxi. The cab pulled up to the condo—how long the walk, how short the ride. I paid and we got out.

"I'm going to sleep," he said. He grabbed a bottle of wine, a glass and a corkscrew, and walked toward his bedroom. "If Dylan and Alex come, tell me about it in the morning. And why don't you call Joe and ask him to take us fresh-water fishing. I've had enough of the ocean."

"Sure," I said. "Good night."

"Goodnight," he replied, and went into his bedroom.

I called Joey and made the arrangements. He knew that Siegel had disembarked.

I took a long hot shower and went to sleep. It was nice not sleeping in a chair. I thought of Harper and stuck to one Ambien. That and two Percosets would do the trick. I'd had enough ocean for awhile.

When I woke up, Doug was making coffee. He was packing a bag with his laptop and an extra bottle of wine.

We walked outside. Joey pulled up and looked at our gear. "That's okay," he said. "We'll travel light." He took my keys and put our stuff in the condo.

We got in the car, me in the front and Doug in the back. He started working on his laptop.

We soon got to some pretty country. The fields were starting to bloom. Numerous streams flowed over the land, over the few hills and many meadows. I looked back to talk to Doug and thought better of it.

I looked out the window. The white houses and motels and glass and steel edifices had a certain poetry when you looked at them from a distance.

Joey parked the car on the side of the road and pulled out the rods and reels and handed them to me. He took out a cooler, a container for bait, and a few other items.

He directed us to a sandy path. We walked into the woods and found two paths, one clear and well-trodden, the other dusty, twisted. We chose the one less traveled.

Muted light filtered through the trees. Patches of ivy sprawled across the ground, interspersed with bare areas of no vegetation. It was lovely and soft, with an air of something old and foreign, as though some ancient travelers had stopped here, leaving a gift of growing things.

I bowed my head to pay deference to those who had passed before. I felt history at my feet.

Doug must have felt the same as he said, "It's magnificent."

Joey picked up the pace.

We could see a larger stream, its water strongly flowing along. In the distance a sparkling lake, surrounded by trees and bushes, contrasted with the few houses with rickety-looking decks, unpainted rowboats with the oars in their locks, and even a few canoes. It was quiet and peaceful and safe. The purity of the air made the lake appear closer than it was. Joe sped along and we trudged behind him.

The pellucid water reflected the sky and houses and docks. Shadows of fish, many fish. I savored the beauty and purity and isolation, and above all, the silence.

"Glaciers created this lake and many more. They're kettle holes that got filled with fish. People don't know it, but the fresh water fishing is fantastic. It's too cold for wading but the canoes at the dock are fine. It's okay, a friend of mine owns the house. He isn't around once summer ends," Joe said.

"What kinds of fish are there?" I asked.

"Perch, crappie, small mouth bass, largemouth bass, blue gills and if we're lucky, wall-eyed pike."

"The walk was worth it."

"I hope so."

"I think I'll sit on the dock and get some work done. Why don't the two of you fish? "Doug said.

Joe went into the house. He brought out a thick blanket and a large thermos of coffee. He handed them to Doug. "It's going to be cold here. Give us a call if you change your mind about fishing."

We got into the rowboat and set off.

Doug was struggling to get closer to the water, getting on his hands and knees. He took out two bottles of wine from his bag and reached into the water, wedging the wine in between the strips of wood of the dock.

He had trouble getting up. Doug was a man in purgatory as he got up from the dock, first on two knees and one hand and standing slowly, using the dock railing for support. He half limped to a chair and sat down clumsily. He wrapped the blanket Joey had given him around himself. He shook his hands in an effort to dry them. He stuck them under the blanket and huddled in the chair. This was my frightening vision of Doug, and all for two bottles of chilled wine.

Joey and I rowed out to the middle of the lake and stopped. I wanted to photograph the magnificence of panoramic view. I took picture after picture.

Joey waited patiently until I put my camera down. He handed me a can of bait. I took a worm and put it on my line. Joey turned on his old fashioned Walkman, which he had connected to two little speakers. The soothing sounds of John Coltrane poured out. This busboy had a lot to him.

A shimmering light of pure silver played with the reflections in the water. It was cold, but we had come well-prepared and wore warm clothing.

I cast out over the lake. I wasn't paying complete attention and didn't realize at first that a fish was on my line. The fish wiggled and was gone.

These were old fish. Their girth and their length was proof of that. These were large. That meant that they had a great deal of experience. I would have to be on my guard. Focus, I told myself, focus.

Joe handed me another rod, already baited. He seemed disappointed in me. I knew one lost fish does not a fishing trip make. The next time a fish bit I was ready and didn't hesitate. It put up a good fight. Joe was ready with the net, thinking I needed help.

Thus, I got my first fish from that lake, an old fish from another time. Many more followed. It took a while to get bored of having a multitude of fish wanting to come into the boat, but all good things come to an end.

We paddled back to the dock. Doug came to meet us.

"How did you do?"

"It was fine. Good day fishing."

Doug took a last slug of his wine and walked toward the car.

Joey packed up the fish and the gear, waving me off when I tried to help. We headed toward the car. When you drive anywhere, the way back always seems shorter. Walking is another story. The path seemed sandier, the trees taller, and the air darker and heavier.

It was still early when we got back.

As we got out of the car, Joe seemed as though he wanted to say something.

"What is it, Joe," I asked.

"Mr. Gosling, could I ask you a personal question?"

"Sure," Doug said.

"What is it like to be so famous?"

"Fame, before I had it, was what I wanted most. The sad thing is, I've learned what's important, and it's not fame, but I still want it. When I write, it's all about the writing. A great writer brings a reader into a new, and truer, universe. I don't believe writers have more pain than other people, but they express it better. I just try to make sense of my feelings. It's raw and it's real and only a few of us can do it," Doug said. "But I don't do it directly. That's the flaw of the untalented. I never cheat my readers. I channel my despair. If I describe a sunset, my readers see the sunset through tears or laughter. Just saying, I feel lousy or I feel great isn't art. I'm a hopeless romantic and think I could be in love, but I'm also a realist and I know I can't be. I'm so flawed.

"When I'm writing, the inner conflict between good and bad becomes tangible. Inhibitions disappear, and all that matters is the discovery. It's not teaching. I issue no proclamations, or if I do, they're misdirections, and false, for what I proclaim I am is precisely what I am not."

Doug stopped for a moment and then said, "People don't know me. I'm not my writing, and never was, except maybe in my earliest stories. I don't want to be known or understood anymore, but I still have that inexorable need to be loved. But as for fame, it just means people want to take a piece of you and you have to become hard or there'll be nothing left."

Doug and I got out of the car and walked into the condo.

Siegel, Dylan and Alex were maintaining radio silence. Before going to sleep, I took an Ambien and went to the outdoor shower and rinsed myself with hot water. Ambien and hot showers before bed were becoming a habit.

You practiced a good habit a hundred times and you didn't make it your own, but as for the bad habits, you did them once, and you owned them forever. I fell asleep. That made it a good night.

Doug stumbled into my room in the morning, unshaven and looking rough.

"Good morning," I said.

"Don't rub it in. This came last night." He handed me his phone and showed me the email, which I chose not to read.

"Oh," I asked. "Did someone die?"

"Our fishing trip."

"I think it died last night. I'm ready to go."

"Me too. What's the story?

"They're in Aspen. We're welcome to join them, but there's no room where they are. All their love, and sorry about the change in plans."

"I wonder where Bernie is."

"Doubt it's Aspen."

"His mother has a place there. She's had it for years."

"My, my. He does have money."

"His mother does, which isn't the same thing," I said. "What do you want to do?"

"I don't know. I want to get out of here. I feel like we're in the Twilight Zone, where every day is the same as yesterday, and we can't get out of this condo."

"What was that Buñuel movie, *Avenging Angel*?"

The phone rang. We both reached for it. It was Joe.

"We're heading back to the city this morning. It's time to move on," I said.

"I'll take you to the train station. Be there in a few," Joe said.

When I hung up the phone, I said, "Let's head back to Manhattan, pick up some ski clothes and get a plane to Aspen."

"Sure, it's good out there," Doug said.

Joe was there a few minutes later. We loaded up the car and were on our way.

"Joe, thanks again for everything. We'll call you the next time we're out here."

"I've really enjoyed fishing with you," Joey said. He pulled out two of Doug's books and a cover I had done for *Sports Illustrated*.

"Would you sign these for me, please?"

We obliged.

Joe reached into his back pack and pulled out two packages, and handed one to each of us. I opened the one he gave me and saw six handmade flies.

"This is too much," I said.

"It's the least I could do," Joe said.

Doug opened his package and looked at his six flies.

"I know how competitive you guys are. I made them the same," Joe laughed.

As we got out of the car my phone rang. It was Dylan. Usually nothing made me happier than to hear her voice, but I decided I wasn't ready to be miserable. I didn't answer.

Chapter 16

When we got to Penn Station, it was easy enough to get a taxis, Doug to a hotel, me to my apartment.

I had several crucial dilemmas: bath or shower, delivery or out to dinner, call Dylan, Alex or Turk. I decided on a long bath and no phone calls, putting off the food decision until later. I was surprised Siegel hadn't called, but I had no desire to call him. I didn't call my doctor either. I figured no news was good news.

I went to meet Doug at P.J. Clarks, on 55th and 3rd. We ate cheeseburgers with extra cheese, fries and onion rings, and drank ice-cold beer in chilled glasses.

A good-looking woman sauntered by and saw Doug, stopping to give him a big hug before walking away.

"Ah, that woman. I was sure I was in love with her. Every time I saw her, she had Ecstasy with her. One time she forgot the Ecstasy, and I realized I didn't even like her," Doug said.

Rusty Baron strolled past our table with Supreme Court Justice Esposito. He gave the Judge a big hug. Esposito left and Baron joined our party.

"I'm surprised you're so friendly with Judge Esposito."

"That scoundrel," Rusty said. "I've known him forever and he's greatly indebted to me."

"Why?" I asked.

"A long time ago he came to the fair city of Jackson, Mississippi, to try a case against the Catholic Church and a naughty priest. I welcomed him and gave him what input I could, about the court, the judge, the jury pool. We were much younger and quite a bit less wise. I was between marriages at the time. About two weeks into the trial, he made contact with one of the jurors. She was very beautiful for a juror. He was planning to take her out that night. I told him that the court system down here frowned on that type of thing. He said she had a rather homely friend and if I would accompany them, he would owe me forever.

"I thought, rightfully so, that he was going places and it's always a good thing to be owed one. I prepped for the evening, six shots of jack followed by a beer chaser. By the time the juror and her friend Igor got there, I was sufficiently obliterated. Our learned Chief Judge left with his juror after about five minutes of voir dire-ing. I was drunk and restless so I took my creature back to the hotel. After, I was no longer drunk and had a foul taste in my mouth. I went into the bathroom and drank a glass of water, which she surprisingly and thoughtfully left for me by the sink. When I returned to bed, she got up and went into the bathroom."

Rusty was sort of chuckling to himself, laughing at the memory of something that had happened a long time ago. "She came out fuming, complaining that I'd drunk her contact lenses. When she turned the lights on, I saw what she really looked like, sans makeup. I wished I had swallowed my own spectacles rather than her contact lenses."

"What happened next?" I asked.

"Judge Esposito got an outstanding verdict and continued on with his storied career. A toast to justice," he said.

I raised my glass and caught Rusty staring at my hands.

"I've never noticed those scars before. Are they from the war?" he asked.

"No," said Doug. "Petey here survived a plane crash. That means he's luckier than most. A nine-year-old girl was on fire and Pete put the flames out using his bare hands. Grace under pressure, a real hero. Got him the key to the city, although it was only Cleveland."

"There was a fire extinguisher two feet away which I didn't see. Not so calm, I guess," I said.

"Heroes are made, not born. Had you seen it, you'd be a silly old chap who used a fire extinguisher. Heroes are romantic. Nothing romantic about spraying a chemical. No scars. Heroes need scars."

"I'm a lot of things. Hero isn't one of them."

We drank into the night. I was home safely in bed by three. I slept well.

In the morning, I hustled plane tickets and a place to stay. I checked the weather and found conditions were good. I texted and emailed Dylan and Alex: "Doug and I are coming to Aspen. Staying at the Little Nell. Fishing was great. Hope to see you."

I kept thinking of the laws of inertia. Bodies in motion tended to stay in motion. Bodies at rest tended to stay at rest. That's why we always had to keep going.

I didn't feel like talking to Doug. I emailed him the hotel information. He texted that he would meet me at the hotel. I guessed he too wanted space.

I got to the airport in plenty of time. I went through security and sat in a bar near the gate. I ordered a coke and looked at my pictures.

A tinny voice announced that my plane was boarding. I gave my ticket to the agent, walked through the door and down the hallway to the plane.

I felt rushed. I sat down in a seat in first class, enjoying all of the superior little services. Life had changed since I had first visited Aspen. Now, anybody who was anybody chartered a private plane.

This plane was old and had that funny smell that old planes had—too many trips, too many passengers. The flight attendants were surly, as shop-worn as the plane.

I refused the first offer of a drink on general principles. A fleeting thought, more a wish, hit me. Dylan would meet me at the plane—a yearning, a craving, a desire destined never to be fulfilled. If Dylan met me at the plane, it would be because she was getting ready to go someplace else on that plane.

I sat in the frayed leather seat, eyes closed, more sober than I'd been in years. I realized that Dylan had never betrayed my trust because I'd never trusted her.

The best thing about Dylan was that she never pretended to be other than what she was. She might have to change when she got older and lost her looks, but not yet, not now.

The pilot told us to look out the window to see some beautiful scenery, just as we were beginning our final descent. I sat in the seat, with my eyes closed. I knew Aspen, snow, mountains, and beautiful blue skies. I wasn't in the mood for scenery.

In the terminal I ran into two French extreme skiers whom I vaguely remembered.

Their latest idea was to trigger an avalanche at the top of a mountain and then make their run. They strapped on helmet-cams so the viewer knew how it felt to ski down a mountain with a mass of snow barreling down behind you.

Years ago, they had asked me to do a feature on them, but the time had never been right. Manmade danger never filmed well. The pictures demonstrated that the skiers shouldn't have been there in the first place.

ESPN had been pushing me for more stories. I made a quick call and got the go-ahead.

I looked at the Frenchmen, one tall and slim, the other short and wiry, two well-built, athletic-looking crazy men. I smiled at them and they smiled back, smiles getting warmer as they recognized me.

"So, are you up for adventure?" one of them asked.

"I can photograph you tomorrow, weather permitting," I said.

"Good," they replied. They gave me details, which I entered into my phone, and asked if I needed a ride.

Bernie Siegel stood by the gate. He saw me and walked over. I thanked the Frenchmen and told them I'd see them that night.

Bernie smiled and took my bag.

For one brief second I wondered if Dylan was there.

"I'm parked outside," Bernie said. "Sorry I left Montauk without an explanation."

I didn't tell him we were happy to see him go.

He half ran to the car and shoved my stuff in the back, jumping around the car and getting in on the driver's side. He was in a hurry and even more nervous than usual.

The air was crisp and clean. "They're out skiing, or else shopping, or lunching, or something. They've stopped texting me or answering my calls," he said, looking straight ahead, not looking at me, not looking at the sky.

"Well, that's a message right there," I said. "It was nice of you to pick me up. You want to stop someplace for a drink?"

He shook his head. "Wouldn't mind some lunch, though. My mother's chef's brisket is something everyone should have at least once before they die."

"I'll have to take you up on that some other time. I really want to check in. I'd like to get settled."

"No problem. I have to pick some stuff up at my mother's. It's on the way."

"Sure," I said, annoyed.

"It's right on Buttermilk, just outside of Aspen. It's got great views. It really will be just a minute."

I knew Siegel's mother had property all over the world, which his father had left her. Siegel's father, a notorious womanizer, owned and managed several hotels and casinos in Nevada. His wife and son lived in Montana. This was not a good thing for Bernie, because he bore the full brunt of his mother's craziness. After accumulating a vast fortune, Bernie's father returned to Montana and spent the rest of his life revising his past. Like many others before him, he became a philanthropist, and if not rendering his reputation white as snow, it was no longer as black as it had been. Time does repaint the past in softer hues.

We drove up to the house. It was a very grand house on a splendid lot. We got out of the car and I stood, transfixed. I wanted to take pictures of the panorama, of the mountains and valleys, of the clouds that looked just like the ocean; surf sweeping over the tops of maintains and painting trees in foggy hues. A creek meandered through the property, surrounded by wildflowers and soft bushes.

Siegel let himself in. We walked into the three-story-high foyer, with its large mission glass windows. Distinct views could be seen from each window. An indoor-outdoor swimming pool and tennis courts loomed in the distance.

"I'll just go upstairs. It won't take a minute," Bernie said.

I walked over to a polished black Steinway grand piano and sat on an intricately carved bench covered by an antique needlepoint cushion. I played a few notes.

On the piano stood pictures of a smiling family. The incandescent smiles of the children bespoke protection and trust. It was all a lie and the piano was out of tune.

Siegel held a pair of ski boots in one hand. He half dragged me out of the house with his other hand.

"I never knew your father was such a handsome man," I said.

"Yes, Mr. Wonderful. He was great. His best quality was that he only cheated when he had to. Let's get out of here. "

We quickly got into Siegel's car and he peeled out of the driveway.

"You want to ski?" he asked.

"Tomorrow is fine."

Skiing at high altitudes meant burning lungs, but it was worth it. It was all fresh powder, whooshing sounds, almost gliding, almost flying.

I didn't know why I didn't want to get to the slopes. I would have bet that Dodo skied well. I was sure he skied often. Doug would be fine in the morning. Alex would be solid, but better before the booze. Dylan would watch, maybe ski, and look great, graceful and smooth. Every eye would be on her.

She constantly spoke about the pressure of being herself, how people expected so much. The truth was she sought the limelight, sought the attention, craved it, and moved on.

I pulled my phone out of my pocket. No messages. I put the phone back in my pocket.

"Go ahead. Call her," Siegel said.

"I'll wait."

Siegel laughed. "For all you know, they left Colorado last night or this morning, on to some new place, some new people. At least I've had the chance to do some skiing. Have you skied Highland since they added the new lift? Half a mile of vertical terrain—fantastic skiing."

"Nope, haven't been there in years. The hike made it better, I think. The long hike kept everyone away," I told him.

"I've been writing about skiing. My novel is going well. I've been doing a lot of thinking too. There are so many women here that it's a little hard to concentrate. When the women are so accessible, they're a lot less attractive," Siegel said.

"What do you think makes a woman desirable?" I asked.

"She has to be unattainable."

I laughed a hard laugh.

Siegel left me, presumably to ski. In Aspen, you ski, you drink, you go to the spa. Some of the women did a lot of shopping. No matter what your choice, you ended up in a Jacuzzi or a well-heated pool, you drank, and you talked. If you were smart, it was after skiing.

Chapter 17

After I checked in, I confirmed the avalanche shoot with my editor and called the French guys. They said I should eat dinner with them and sleep at their base camp because they were going to ski very early.

I spent a little time on the slope—an hour or two—then took a nap and went up to the Frenchmen's base camp. The camp had igloos and tents and a roaring fire. People were sitting around the blaze, smoking and drinking beer. I could hear the wings of birds fluttering in the distance and wondered why birds would be up so high.

The leaves were rustling gently, promising a soft, quiet morning, good for the adventure ahead. Suddenly, we saw a hang glider lit up with Christmas lights, swooping down below us.

Music played. I heard the Doors and thought of sitting at Jim Morrison's grave. Better to have lived intensely, to have created something truly grand, than trudge into old age, disappointed and alone, I thought.

When I settled in, I saw an elderly gentleman, a prominent physician, who had been our next-door neighbor when I was a child. I watched the snow crunching under the heavy boot of the old man, which left proof of where he'd been. The new snow would quickly destroy the evidence of his journey.

My mother had hated him because she suspected that he'd poisoned our dog, a venerable mutt, a cross between a Terrier, Labrador, and Shepherd, who'd lived to the ripe old age of eleven and died suddenly. When you're two thousand miles away from home, seeing a familiar face is always comforting, like a glass of chocolate milk before bed, even if the guy had killed your dog. I watched his figure, the large green jacket and fur rimmed hood, disappear into the dark and snow concomitantly.

I was here to take a picture and he, a trauma surgeon, to provide medical assistance in case something went wrong.

What are the odds of a seventy-year-old physician and thirty-year-old photographer, who used to be neighbors, meeting two thousand miles away to take part in an imbecilic ski run. In this case, 100 percent.

The Frenchmen had swag. They drank heavily that night, vodka, rum, brandy. One of them left with two women. It's good to have swag.

I went to the tent assigned to me and slept fitfully until the morning's first light.

Human beings run from danger. It's the most basic of instincts. Freud called it the flight instinct. As a photographer we head toward danger. It's an opportunity. When I was at war I confronted danger because I had to. I was frightened and miserable but tried my best to be brave. I always wanted to be a man of action. Now I just take pictures of men of action. It's very derivative.

In the morning we woke up. Off we went. It was beautiful at the top of the mountain and the powder was sublime. I skied down looking straight ahead, enjoying the silence and the cold, crisp air, and marking the areas of bushes and trees. Except for a few large boulders, the terrain was snow.

I turned, resting myself against a tree, and heard a large chopping noise. I saw them use a parachute apparatus as they jumped down onto the snow. I started skiing backwards and watched as the snow came barreling after them. They were coming close to me as I—hypnotized—continued to snap pictures until I heard them yelling.

"Turn around. Turn around. Get the hell out of here."

I knew they cared more about my pictures than my safety, but I twisted around and, with a jump, got the hell out.

We skied the rest of the way down the mountain without mishap. I was exhilarated and exhausted and aware that what I had done was stupid and dangerous and fantastic.

At lunch, eating hot soup and fresh baked bread, I looked over the pictures, which were outstanding. I even had video, which came out well. I told my companions that I would submit the photos to ESPN and email them copies after I got back to New York.

They were a little unpleasant, because they wanted the pictures for their website, which I promised would happen, but not until I completed my business. I don't think they got that this was the way I made my living and that without a payday I wouldn't be skiing down a mountain in front of an avalanche.

It didn't take long to make a photo story of the excitement, which my editor told me was old news. They were good pictures though. The editor used them.

I returned to the hotel and found a message from Doug. He wanted me to meet him in the sauna near the outdoor pool. On the way down I ran into Siegel.

The three of us ended up in the pool with large drinks. Nobody mentioned the fading bruises on my body.

I am not in bad shape, which was what saved my life in Maryland. Doug was flabby. Drink and good living had taken its toll. That laborious effort to right himself on the dock told me how much his body had deteriorated. Siegel was in the same shape he'd been in at eighteen, or maybe in even better shape, because he worked at it more.

The Bloody Marys were good, a divinely inspired creation filled with nourishment, which is important if you're doing serious drinking. They go down a lot easier than solid food.

The three of us sat in the swimming pool at the Little Nell, and drank Bloody Marys and stared at the women walking by. Doug was getting worse. He drank two drinks to each one of ours, and all he got was introspective.

"Good drinking and good sex," he said. "Everything else is just noise."

We were listening to some of the people sitting near us in the pool. It was easier than talking.

"This is the first time I've been at the ski house since my father passed away. I miss the old man," a man who looked to be a hundred said.

"My old man didn't teach me much, which was fine, because he didn't know much," Doug said. "He gave me three simple rules for living your life: never turn down a drink; never, ever, walk away from a fight; and sleep with any woman who will sleep with you. It's no wonder he died alone, a syphilitic drunk with a punched-in face."

I was about to have a revelation about this when a woman slid into the pool with a drink in her hand and a sparkle in her eye. The pool lit up. Dylan smiled. She had that the knack of lighting up a room when she walked in. When she left, the lights dimmed and we all felt sad, but she was here, with no hint of departing, and the sun was shining and the sky was blue and snow was abundant. Life was good.

Hi, chaps," she said. "It's nice to see you again. I adore this place—all these beautiful people."

Every eye in the pool was on Dylan. The preppie smiled at Dylan, confident in his good looks and his money. I wanted Dylan to ignore him. Instead she smiled and gave a welcoming nod of her head.

He half walked, half swam, as he came toward us.

"Hi, Johnny," she said. She turned to us. "This is the skier, Johnny Russek." We all smiled.

Johnny was tall and blond, with a slim waist and no hips and shoulders that could have been surgically enhanced. He wore a lightweight sweatshirt over an abbreviated bathing suit, boxers, not speedos. He leaned against the side of the pool next to Dylan. He brushed his hands inadvertently against her and I knew. You can always tell when people are sleeping together. Nobody's fooling anyone unless they want to be fooled.

"Heaven, my dear Dylan, is seeing you."

Doug had once said that his drinking attracted more interesting people. I guess he didn't realize that alcohol tended to make people seem more interesting—and beautiful. Women who were twos at 10:00 PM became tens at 2:00 AM.

Doug was morose. He put his drink by the side of the pool and said, "Heaven is dying when you're young and healthy and know everyone loves you, when life is possibility and all possibilities seem good. Hell is living in a nursing home, wearing a diaper, smoking a cigar when you only have one lung and thinking you're getting away with something."

Johnny, the blond god, stripped off his T-shirt. His right shoulder was disfigured, a monstrous knot with some bone sticking through. It was difficult to look at.

"Here's what hell is," a boy, no more than twenty-five, said pointing at Johnny's injured arm. "If it were any worse, it would mean no more skiing. No more nothing, feeling like you're going no place and accomplishing nothing."

We watched as Johnny plunged into the water and swam away. His friend followed him—two athletes swimming in tandem, with the image of repulsive ugliness superimposed on beautiful bodies, all the uglier.

Snow came down, not an Irish shroud, a soft blanket muting the idiotic attempts at humor by good looking, well-built, world-class athletes, hiding the devastation caused by too much confidence or maybe some war or some drunken driving incident. It didn't make a difference. The point is, it didn't matter why a catastrophe occurred, it only mattered that it happened.

Someone was buying us drinks, smooth cognac that went down easy. I tried to make it a habit not to mix drinks, but the cognac was too good to pass up.

Skiers were coming in, breaking for lunch. Carved out bread with Swedish meatballs. Swiss fondue with bread cubes, and fruit and sculpted vegetables. A reggae band was playing in the background.

Doug said, "Heaven and hell—an empty place with no one in it but me and my memories. Hell is a lot of alcohol but no matter how much you drink, you never get drunk, or a martini with an olive that's three minutes old and it's right in front of me, and I have no arms and no hands and can't pick it up."

Dylan said, "Heaven is where we all stay young and beautiful forever."

"And hell?" Doug asked.

"Hell?" Dylan replied, eyes softening, "I don't think of ugly things. It's a waste of time."

Ah ... Dylan. I drank more of my cognac. A beautiful, soft cloud floated over the pool, over the people in the pool, over me. It was good. Life was good. I felt that wonderful feeling of ease and comfort, of knowing the world was safe. I didn't have to worry. I didn't have to think. I lazed in the pool and drank my drink and smoked my cigar.

I was ... taken care of.

I remembered Hemingway writing that heaven was two *Barrera* seats in a big bull ring, *en la sombra*, the shady side, with a trout stream outside that was for him and no one else, with two large houses nearby. One would be for his wife and children and he would be faithful and love them all and spend happy times with them. The other would be for his many mistresses. Heaven was a place where the mutually exclusive co-existed, and hell was a place where there were no consequences.

I drank more of the cognac. Hemingway slipped away. Memory slipped away. Cognitive faculties slipped away. It was nice not worrying. Hemingway wrote about critical literary magazines being printed on tissue paper for all the many bathrooms in the house. That was Hemingway, sexist and jejune. He was ironic and funny and didn't take himself seriously, at least not in print. No pity, though—none for others and none for himself.

Well, at least until he shot himself. He had to feel self-pity before he pulled the trigger. Killing yourself is a significant clue to how you take yourself.

A half cackle impinged upon the pleasant buzz. A flat Midwestern accent, another one of the skiers with a great face, a strong body, and little affect. He spoke without emotion. It was eerie. He was a male Barbie doll who thought he was real. It's one thing if children think toys are real, but it's scary when it's a living, breathing male who doesn't know he's fake.

"Heaven is fresh powder, no wind, sunshine, Red Hot Chile Peppers on my iPod and no snowboarders," he said.

Douglas mumbled to himself. "All writers want to be adored. If they can't be loved, they want to be drunk."

"What?" asked one of the young beauties?

Doug looked up, shocked I think, that he had been speaking aloud and that someone had heard him. "I've got to get some sleep. I've been working too hard."

"I love sleep," the young girl said to Doug, not realizing that Doug didn't even notice her existence. Young girls are like that, the good looking ones.

For me, I love drinking. A bunch of people drinking together think they're having a lot of fun. The consequences of the evening are not as much a source of glee, but we don't associate the pain of the late evening with imbibing spirits. That's a connection that we can't see. Our brains are protective of our drinking and malfunction, when necessary, causing us to miss the simple phenomenon of cause and effect.

Another thing about drinking in groups is that you have the intimacy without the discomfort that true intimacy presents, and believe me, for the dysfunctional, true intimacy is a consummation devoutly not to be desired. The beauty of drinking with others was that no one listened, no one at all.

I reached over the side of the pool, pulled my backpack to me, and took a Quaalude. Drinking was good as far as it went, but it inevitably went too far, spiraling into pitiful, incomprehensible demoralization.

I often felt that way. Much as I hated that feeling I couldn't stop drinking. Drugs worked wonders. MDMA, a bump of cocaine, that's heaven, and don't let anyone tell you different.

A flurry of activity signified my friends were on their way— time for more skiing. Dodo had walked up unnoticed by me. He beckoned to Dylan.

"Time to get a move on," she said. She pulled herself out of the pool. The young skiers followed her. Siegel hurried after them. I hadn't seen him. He'd been sitting in a chair near the pool. Poor guy. Poor pathetic guy.

I watched them dry themselves off and put on ski clothes. Johnny became a Nordic God again.

Dylan was in the middle of the pack, as usual. She walked away and they, the pack, walked with her. No farewells. No waves. We were the paper dolls that made up the audience and required no acknowledgement. Sad for them. Sadder for her.

Martin Buber characterized these as "I-It" relationships. It's okay to use other people as objects, but the consequence is that you become an object as well. Martin Buber was a smart man.

Chapter 18

Two dark-skinned short men, wearing the beige uniform of the hotel, were stringing strands of Christmas lights over the pool area. They switched them on to make sure that all the many-colored lights were shining. The men were painstaking in their efforts. No one was around, and still they checked each and every light as though their movements were on film.

Waiters came by asking if we wanted food or something to drink. The Reggae Band played and walked around. A young woman danced to the music. People put money in the pockets of her multi-colored skirt.

One of the night managers came over to the pool. I had met him several years ago. His name was Escobar. He had sung in a similar band once upon a time and cleaned toilets for a living. I wrote about him, hoping to give him a boost.

The hotel promoted him to general maintenance, and rewarded him for his intelligence and his hard work by continuing to promote him until he became, first, the night manager of one of the lesser hotels, and later, here. He had come far from those days.

As I soaked in the pool, Escobar leaned over and shook hands with me in his welcoming way, seeming sincere. He always seemed sincere. It was his stock in trade, but I believed he was pleased to see me.

"Your friends have arrived," he said.

"Yes," I said. "I've seen some of them."

"Dylan and her fiancé and some other people." He smiled as though he had a secret that I would hear about.

"When did they get in?" I asked. I was surprised. I thought they were staying in some megaluxe ski chalet.

"They've been here for a few days. I gave them your favorite rooms."

"Is Mr. Siegel on the same floor?"

"Regrettably, no," he said. "We are crowded. I've put you and Mr. Gosling at the end of the floor, and Mr. Siegel two floors below."

How did he know? How strange that he knew where people belonged. I've spent my whole life trying to figure that out.

"What time are we skiing tomorrow?" I asked.

"You'll start at six. You're skiing with my best guy, Dan Stallings. He wants to talk to you."

"Great, I'm around."

Escobar leaned over, putting his hand on my shoulder. "Good," he said. "It never hurts to be careful."

He smiled again. He always smiled. He made the extreme skiing a special secret between the two of us. We had this secret between us, this need for speed and solitude and danger. It was our dirty little secret and scandalous to outsiders. It wouldn't do to expose it to people who would not understand.

Your friend?" Escobar smiled at Doug.

"He came all the way from New York to do this. He's fit," I said.

"An early night would be wise. No disco. No rum punch."

"*Desde luego,*" I said. "Of course."

"Ah, but he has his sorrows. His sorrows are deadly. The slopes do not allow the luxury of sentimentality. *Cuidado, mi amigo. Cuidado.* Please take care."

He put his hand on my shoulder again, a sign of affection. He nodded his head, straightened, and walked away.

Escobar was American, born in Laredo, Texas. His family was from South America. He was well-educated. Being mistaken for a Mexican must have taken its toll. I never understood how he ended up cleaning toilets in some third-rate hotel or singing in some mediocre band. He must have had secrets he hadn't told me. Escobar was very discreet.

The man was courtly and punctilious. He'd go far in the hotel world. He did not, I think, color outside the lines. Escobar would ski with us tomorrow. How he became a skier is another thing I don't know, but an excellent skier is what he was. I knew he was a good tennis player as well.

Escobar didn't like my friends. They were careless people and didn't act well. Senior managers of luxury hotels were well aware of the habits and predilections of their guests and didn't talk about them.

I sat in the pool, willing myself to get out, sitting there, not eating, not drinking, soaking in the comfort of the warm water.

Doug waded over to me.

"You know," he said, "I'm not going with you tomorrow. It would be insane. Don't know if I ever skied well enough, but I certainly don't now."

My fatigue made speaking impossible. I was weary of egos, weary of fear, weary of ill manners. And yet Doug was being more than prudent, more than cautious. He was right, and I shouldn't be skiing either.

"You'll have plenty of company," Doug said. "I think I'll do some writing, maybe some thinking. Hell I'll even go to Church. I need some absolution." As he got out of the pool, he, too, put a hand on my shoulder, a mockery of Escobar.

"He's taking care of the skiing," I said, referring to Escobar.

"Sure. I need a rest from your crew. They're a lot to take. Say, let's go to Alabama or Spain or anywhere else. Do your skiing and let's get out of here. Write that novel you're always threatening to write. Get a job with a newspaper in a small town."

"Or sail around the world. Buy a farm. Till the soil. Lots of great dreams," I said. "Drinking helps me run away from reality."

I added, "Wasn't it the scholar Shields who said the more you run away from reality the harder it hits you in the head when it catches up with you?"

Doug said, "Shields was a hack."

He looked at me, and walked away.

I got out of the pool and dried myself off. I went to one of the little cabanas, took a quick shower, and put on clean clothes. Everything at this hotel seemed brand new and clean, without a speck of dust or a streaked window.

The minions worked without stopping—the industrious short, stocky men with dark skin, maybe with dreams. Escobar, who had been one of them, managed to escape the hell of minimum wage.

I saw a mini-restaurant off to one side. I sat down and ordered tuna on rye toast and a light beer. It was the best tuna sandwich I'd ever had.

I stared at the beer shining in its tall glass. A toast, I thought, to tuna fish, and laughed. Real drinkers don't make toasts—it's a waste of time. As I looked at the glass of beer, a man came up to me, an older version of the Nordic God, with laugh lines around his eyes and a worried look on his face. He greeted me.

"I'm Dan Stallings.

"Hi. Pete Stanton. There'll be four of us, all good skiers. The guy that Escobar was worried about isn't coming. He decided it would be a mistake."

"That's good. We've had a lot of accidents up there. Things that are good can get bad in an instant."

He was earnest and sincere.

"Listen," I said. "Maybe we should skip this. We've done this before."

"Yeah," he said. "Ski. You might want to rethink this. There's plenty of good skiing. You know, desperation and thrills don't mix—and not with drugs. You guys are a catastrophe waiting to happen."

"We may look like we don't know what we're doing, but all of us can ski really well. Don't be so dramatic."

"I'll take you, but whatever happens, it's on your head."

He slammed a few dollars down for the iced tea he'd had. I sat there, stunned.

I paid for my lunch, got up, and walked away. I've sat at bars for hours but not this time. I went to my room—and got some ski gear. I went to a Double Blue and started skiing.

I thought about all the different kinds of snow, and how the wind created treachery and betrayal, the blizzards, the avalanches. The same slope was new, brand new, even though I had skied this slope many times. I was winded. I was tired. I veered off and started a great run, smooth and straight, straight as a sliced throat.

My arms ached. My legs ached. My ankles locked. This morning's avalanche had more of an effect than I'd thought. I started to ski really fast. I was flying, feeling the hiss of the powder. I wanted to soar up the hills and down the hills. My tired body told me I'd had enough. I had crossed some great divide. It was over. I wasn't so young any more.

I was one more has-been in a world of has-beens. I walked to Dan Stalling, who was sitting at the bar by the pool, drinking a beer. He was easy in his body and strong, as though he were young. I paid him for the helicopter and his expertise. I gave him the money and said goodbye, to him, to my youth, to my dreams.

I thought of Escobar, an estimable guy, someone who had very high standards. He was polite, of course, and none of the skiers knew his true opinion of them. He was a kind man, but merciless. He'd seen the great ones who pursued excellence, and all the others, useless and unwelcome, chum spilled on the water when trying to attract game fish,

I went up to our suite—two bedrooms and a sitting room, with Peter Max prints. A big window looked out on the mountain. The sun was shining, making snow glisten, people shine. I heard the snow crunching as people walked down the paths to the bars, the little restaurants, the pool, the great room in the lobby where people made new friends and betrayed old ones.

Doug was in his room. The lights were out. He was on his bed, a pillow over his head. His shoes were on.

"More info from the busboy?" he asked.

"Look, Escobar is a good guy. Once upon a time I took a picture of him, which made him a local celebrity and helped his career. He's grateful. Unlike most people, he sees gratitude as an action word. What's wrong with that?"

"What's wrong with anything?" Doug asked. "I still say it's time to depart. Let's find the gang and socialize, and then take off after you go skiing.

"Maybe. Decided that Dylan won't fall for you?"

"She likes hanging around assholes."

"Can't argue with that. Not sure Alex is an asshole though."

"The best thing about him is that he knows he's an asshole," Doug said. "You know, I used to avoid assholes."

"Really? I asked.

"Yeah. I gave up on it though. I ended up being alone all the time."

I laughed and asked him if he bought the tickets.

"Yup, two tickets to anywhere. You'll ski with them and we'll move on. Please don't comment on my not drinking. I'm one in a long line of writers who drinks too much. Did you know that in 1939 Hemingway was ordered to cut down on his drinking? He breakfasted on tea and gin, and drank absinthe, whiskey and vodka on a regular basis. That was his cutting down.

"He had diabetes, muscle cramps, sleeplessness, and sexual impotence. He killed himself when he was sixty-two. Faulkner, O'Neill, Fitzgerald, Capote, and who else? Maybe it's the cost of writing, of being stripped bare in front of millions of people. Maybe it's part of imagining a different reality and feeling the pain of getting at the truth. I don't know, but do I know I can't do it anymore. I'll stay here and read. Give my regrets."

He stretched out on his bed, and closed his eyes.

Doug had quit many times before. It never lasted long. He should cut down, not quit cold turkey, I thought.

I went into my backpack and put two Xanax in an envelope and sealed it shut. On the outside of the envelope I wrote 'These will help if you're feeling bad.' I put the packet on his chest.

I picked up the room key and left the suite. I shut the door. I walked to the elevator and went down stairs, thinking of the enormity of his sorrow.

I went to the Ajax Tavern, the happening place where my happening friends would end up. A lot of people ate and drank and laughed, good looking, slender, well-coordinated people with white teeth and shiny hair. I saw Dylan and Alex sitting with Siegel. They had the ruddy complexion of people who'd been skiing. Siegel was decked out in Spyder gear. Dylan had on a Kjus Calibur ski jacket. Alex was in something expensive.

Dodo was there with some young skiers, identical quintuplets. This was the air brushed generation.

On the table were a number of platters with oysters, shrimp, and crab. I saw quiches and beef Tartare, and a few big pitchers of sangría. Everyone was laughing and eating and drinking—and talking. One thing about alcoholics, they tend to talk a lot.

It was a celebration.

Dylan, whose eyes were always looking for the next party and the next big thing, saw me first. She had some reason for acknowledging me, and waved. Her eyes crinkled up as I came to the table.

Otherwise, I was ignored.

I think it was the preppie from the pool, who asked, "Dylan, are you using the hair stuff?"

"Oh please. That's so last year," she said.

I'd heard that Dylan had been paid a lot of money for endorsing some product that lasted until someone asked her if she used it. It must have been a lot of money but not enough.

"Whatever," she'd said. "They wanted me to give back the money. That wasn't happening."

"As long as it's not a lawsuit, darling," Alex said.

Dylan looked annoyed.

"Hello, Pete. It's good to see you."

Dylan smiled. She was glad to see me.

Alex had a way of getting an intensity of feeling into shaking hands. Bernie Siegel shook hands firmly, as he'd been taught, but with no warmth. He was a wax statue at Madame Tussaud's, or maybe a windup toy.

That was why he was having so much trouble now. Everybody had a different idea as to what he should do, although leaving would have pleased most of them. That was the one thing he wouldn't do.

"Where the hell have you guys been? " I asked. "What happened to our fishing trip on Long Island?"

"There's no decent fishing on Long Island, summer or winter," Alex said. "How did it go?"

"You missed a good thing," I told him. "Didn't Siegel tell you?"

"Was it worth going out to the end of Long Island?" Alex asked."

"Yes. Good fishing. The fish had fight in 'em. It was ideal.

"Good fishing," Siegel said.

We all ignored him.

The waiter came by two or three times, substituting full pitchers for the empties. He took away the food. Good as it looked, no one was eating it.

Dodo paid for the food. He nodded at me, acknowledging my presence for the first time. I nodded and walked away, Dylan at my side. Siegel walked along with us, out the door, past the pool and outside. It was good to be outside.

Dodo and Alex followed. The air was crisp and cool. The sky was alight with thousands of stars. The Reggae band was back.

I remembered my own garage band. These guys were pros compared to us. A different lifetime. We were innocent, naïve, and full of hope.

We walked through the town of Aspen, enjoying the beauty of the women, the masculine good looks of the men. We passed an upscale liquor store. A sign, Fine Wines and Liquors, hung in the window. No sign blaring Girls, Girls, Girls. The discreet offering of good wines at reasonable prices was more in keeping with the Aspen aesthetic.

They'll have some decent wines," Alex said, coming up behind us.

"Nothing special, but not terrible," Dodo said.

A man and a woman argued on the street in front of a jewelry store. They went silent and stared at Dylan.

We walked on.

"Have you ever skied at night?" Dodo asked me.

"When I was a kid, I skied all the time. We all did. We were fearless. Dumb. You?"

"Neither dumb nor fearless," he answered. "We skied at night to avoid the patrols. It worked. We'll start tomorrow morning before first light."

He walked on.

"Did you ski when you were a kid? Were you a star athlete?" Alex asked Siegel.

"I played some football. I wrestled. I wasn't bad," Siegel said.

"When did you become the spare tire with a flat?" Alex asked.

I was embarrassed.

Dylan laughed a fake tinkling laugh. I was becoming disenchanted. Bernie Siegel was angry—his face flushed, his eyes hard. Dodo maintained his placid expression, bored by it all.

Alex persisted, "You're the last action hero, Bernie. Doesn't that mean you should do something?"

"Pearls before swine," Bernie muttered.

"Oh come on. Earn your keep. Be amusing. Let's have a good time." Alex was relentless.

"Be quiet Alex," Dylan said.

"Why don't you say something, Bernie? Why not stand up for yourself. Say something, anything."

"Maybe someone should sing *Amazing Grace*. Oh no, wrong religion. *Havana Gila*. So what if Dylan slept with you?"

"Alex, enough," Siegel said. "Enough?"

"Oh yeah? Are you going to hit me?"

"No one wants you here, except maybe your wife, because you're not there. Don't you get it? No one wants you. It's time for you to pack up your stuff and go home. Get it? We would say, oh good, that Siegel fellow is gone, but you won't be missed."

"Shut up. You're drunk," Siegel said.

"Enough, Alex," I said.

"Where is your pride? Get it through your sick head that it's over. No, there's nothing to be over, you were a convenience, a Portapotty. Nobody likes to use them but sometimes you have no other choice. Why don't you get out of here and go with your own kind," Alex said.

"Come on Bernie," I said, putting my arm around his shoulder. He was vibrating with tension.

"Oh, don't go, Bernie. Isn't it your turn to buy us a drink?" Alex sneered.

I tried to pull Bernie away. Alex kept on talking. Dylan looked disgusted. Bernie shrugged my arm off. His face was green. I thought he'd throw up. He walked out.

"That was awful, Alex. Was it necessary?" Dylan asked.

"Yes," Alex said.

"On the other hand, you weren't wrong. And at least we got rid of the pest," she said.

"Good riddance," Alex said.

Dylan laughed. "Alex Bank, you're very drunk. I thought he would hit you."

"I'm not drunk."

"Of course not," Dylan said.

"I didn't say anything I didn't mean. He's an ass. Dylan uses people. They move on."

Dodo, who had been speaking on a cell phone all this time, gave Dylan and me a goodnight salute, and looked malevolently at Alex. Dylan smiled at him. He bowed to us all and left.

"What's got his knickers twisted?" Alex asked.

"Do you think this stuff is palatable?" I asked.

"Oh please. Dodo has seen worse," Alex said.

"I wonder what Siegel's book is about. I never read it," Dylan said.

I told her it got good reviews. I hadn't read it either, although I had tried.

"I've read all of Doug's books. He's great. He is one good writer," I mused.

"Do you think Siegel will come back?" Dylan asked.

"Like a bad penny," Alex said. "Of course he'll come back. Someone should tell him to man up. Otherwise, we'll have more of these scenes. I can't take the scenes, you know."

"You can't take them," Dylan said. "You create them."

As I heard Alex jabbering, I remembered high school. I had an old girlfriend who had cheated on me and kept it a secret. She finally came clean and broke up with me. I would have preferred that she kept on lying. I guess I hadn't changed much after all.

We finished off the rest of the sangría.

Dylan and Alex walked back to the hotel together, the two of them, arm in arm, snuggling close together. I walked behind and heard a woman singing *Strange Fruit*.

Shades of Billie Holiday. The woman wasn't bad... *"scent of magnolias sweet and fresh, the sudden smell of burning flesh."*

I kept walking.

Chapter 19

When I got back to the Hotel, Escobar was sitting in a chair in the lobby, waiting up for me.

"Your friends have gone to bed. That Mr. Siegel, he didn't look good. He's in his room now. The lady and Mr. Bank are upstairs as well. He's not the right man for her—too angry. She needs a gentle touch, but firm," Escobar said.

"She needs something," I said.

"Thank you again for the skiing, Mr. Pete. Is there anything you need tonight? No? We will have a good day tomorrow."

I went up to the suite. Douglas was sprawled on the couch, watching a basketball game.

"Siegel stopped in for a minute. He looked green," Doug said.

"It was awful. Alex was outrageous. He doesn't hold his liquor well. Or maybe he does. He uses being drunk as an excuse to say whatever he wants. Siegel was a fool to come here, but Alex was brutal."

"Siegel should have hit him."

"He deserves it," I said.

"He just doesn't get it. I thought you said Siegel was clever."

"Not clever enough to keep away," I said. "How are you feeling?"

"So far, so good. Sober three hours and feeling fine. Do you have a sleeping pill?"

"Sure."

I gave him two. He swallowed them without water.

"Are you serious about leaving tomorrow? There's a plane at 6:00 P.M."

"Perfect."

"Okay," Doug said, as he went into his room.

"Good night," I said, thinking again of *Strange Fruit*, which was a bizarre song. I went to bed and fell asleep.

The next thing I knew I heard a knocking at the door. It was Dylan. Five minutes later Alex showed up, acting as though nothing had happened. Perhaps nothing had happened.

Alex had ordered from room service, more than enough food for us all. He was sure that we would fall in with his wishes, Dylan's wishes, their wishes, sure of his dominance in our little group. He turned on the TV and found a music station that played light classical pap.

Doug came out of his room, awakened by the music and the knocking of the room service waiter. No one drank, mindful of the next day's skiing.

Doug was manic and funny. He talked about the first girl he'd ever slept with. "You know what she said, 'Don't think this is any affirmation of your good looks or charm. It's a function of cheap alcohol and slim pickings.'"

He kept going. "You know what a perfect husband is. One of my wives told me a perfect husband has one hundred million dollars, a blind eye, a slow wit, and two weeks to live.

"I don't get all the fuss about gay marriages. Let them have a go at it, I say. For me, marriage should be a ten-year contract with five-year options to renew."

Doug was on a roll. "I don't know who said this, maybe one of my wives. 'No woman is ever satisfied because no man has a chocolate penis that shoots out money.'"

Alex tried to interject his own thought, but Doug continued. "Did you know that Edward Delbert said a man wants a virgin who's a whore?"

"Listen," Doug said, "When you're looking to meet a woman in a bar, always look for someone who smokes. If she's dumb enough to smoke, she's dumb enough to sleep with you."

THE URGENCY OF NOW

We all laughed as Doug added, "We writers have an outlet barred to those of more active pursuits. We get to castigate those who reject us. Quite often greatness comes from being petty."

Alex said, "It might be good writing, but it's limiting. It would have to be imperfect and shallow."

"Tell that to all the Hemingway scholars," I said.

"They're limited and shallow too," Alex said, as he took a swallow from his drink.

Doug made jokes about everyone and everything. Alex chimed in, sounding amusing, although when you thought about what he said, he wasn't funny at all. Together they made us all laugh.

I had a meal like this the day before my Humvee exploded. Those were tense times and we were nervous, with good reason. Four guys died and the rest ran away and left me behind. I only survived because two Marines were separated from their unit. United States Marines don't abandon their comrades, even if they're soldiers and not fellow Marines.

On the night of that meal and this night, I felt happy, that everything would be okay. You would think that by this time I would have known better.

Doug went to his room, and Alex and Dylan left my room. I turned off the TV, and went to bed.

A clock glowed on the night table and on the cable box. I paid no attention. I took a long shower, thinking how different this was from my New York apartment. I appreciated the expensive shampoo and conditioner, the perfumed soap, and the endless hot water.

I don't remember much more. I got out of the shower and took a couple of pills, playing my idiosyncratic Russian Roulette—not looking at which pills I took from the single bottle I had reserved for this pastime. Ah yes, this was the true American national past time, suicide by boredom. I remembered putting on the fluffy white bathrobe that all luxury hotels put in your rooms. Many unsuspecting people packed the bathrobes when they left.

Enabling, I thought. You thought you were putting something over on the hotel, until you looked at your credit card statement three or four months later. How many people looked at their credit card statements?

I stood out on the balcony. It wasn't late. People were walking about below. I was on the fourth floor. I stood there for a long time. I came inside and turned off all the lights, except for a dim light over the chair near my bed.

I sat in the chair and tried to read Siegel's book. I read the dedication page over and over again. He dedicated the book to his old boxing coach. It wasn't much of a dedication, but it sounded sincere. Doug had written five remarkable books, each of which was dedicated to a different woman.

The lone exception was *Sodom and Gomorrah Played Vaudeville*, which he dedicated to his son. He won a Pulitzer for the book. I think he'll get a Nobel Prize as well. That's how good a writer he is.

I leafed through Siegel's book but couldn't find a single sentence that touched me. The book was sententious and serious, without Siegel's knockout punch.

As I looked around the room, the fog in my brain lessened. Things became clearer to me. The feeling of heaviness in my upper extremities and head lessened. I was lightheaded. I wanted to go to sleep, but I couldn't close my eyes. Every time I did, the room spun around, and I felt as though I would fall down. I tried to get up from the chair and couldn't.

I decided to reread *Sodom and Gomorrah Played Vaudeville*. I never got past the dedication. It was as good as a tribute to a dying child could be. I took off the bathrobe and threw it over my head. Later, I was able to reach down and unplug the light. I heard people outside, walking by the room. It was still early. Some kids ran by. I thought of Doug's son, alone in a quiet grave.

Sometimes I forgot what my body was doing to me. This time life slowed down to a crawl, inching forward, bit by bit, with each pain-filled moment a private horror.

I managed to call the front desk and ask for medical help, which came very quickly.

Dylan walked in, distraught, disheveled, and positively beautiful. She didn't notice the two guys from the hotel examining me.

"Oh Peter, it was so terrible. They treated me like somebody's mother. I was invisible to these twenty year olds. I'm not that much older than that. They looked at the space where I stood and saw nothing! What do I do? What do I do? I'm Janis Joplin in San Francisco—a prostitute that can't even give it away."

One of the guys stared at her in disbelief. The other didn't seem to notice she was there. I couldn't speak. I was just very tired, very weak. They instructed me to stay hydrated. I wanted to introduce her. 'Here's Dylan. She's the lady who goes to a hospice and complains about having a cold.' I wanted to hate her, or even me.

She might identify if someone had gained a few pounds or had a bad hair day, but she had nothing in her to care about someone with cancer. How pathetic. I yearned for this beautiful creature, a woodland nymph with no soul even as I knew that she had no feelings for me and no feelings for anything in the world unless it gave her what she wanted.

I thought wisdom came with dying. All that comes with dying are fetid smells and horrible pain and the sadness that you realize you've learned nothing in your entire life.

How foolish I had been, believing in my distorted memory of a perfect love. Goodbye to memories. Goodbye to wasted dreams. My life was chalk and ashes, a monument to those who couldn't love and died trying.

I woke up at 3:00 AM and everyone was gone. I was in my bed and felt pretty good, just a little foggy.

I heard howling from outside. I got out of my bed and opened the balcony door. A man wearing ragged clothes stood outside, preaching to a few stragglers getting ready to go to bed.

He spoke in a firm, loud voice.

We value the worthless and think it holy. We are lost but can be found. I will tell you who is blessed, and they've always been blessed but you have forgotten: The poor in spirit, those who mourn, the gentle, those who hunger and thirst for righteousness, those who are merciful, pure in heart. The peacemakers, the persecuted in the name of righteousness, those who are insulted and hurt for believing the truth. Have joy. Be glad, for you are in a long line of others who have been blessed.

I am not here to abolish the Law or those called holy but to fulfill. We are good not for what we have not done, for the crimes we have not committed nor the sins we have not performed, but for the good we have done, the love we have given and the truth we have told.

We must look to behaving well always, of speaking well of others, or not speaking at all, of paying all debts even if they not be known. Our law is not the law of Men. It is truly a higher law and requires much more but also requires nothing. When we love a woman, we love her as a child of God and not an object to be used-for when we treat another as an object, we become an object ourselves.

We must love all, enemies and friends, for to love only those who love us is narrow and, indeed wrong. The sun shines on the good and evil alike. In hating we become the hated. We do not practice goodness to be noticed or admired or praised. Let your actions be your prayers. The greatest action is love of others, not through sacrifice of self but through the sharing of self.

I realized this was the Sermon on the Mount speech from *God Went Fishing*.

The man made good progress before three men wearing Aspen Police Department uniforms approached him. They were a triangle moving in on the drunk in a practiced way. It took about five seconds before one of them grabbed him, pushed his face into the chest of the second man, and held it there. The man's preaching was not even a murmur.

They half-carried him into a waiting police car and took him away without disturbing anyone but, I think, me. There is precious fruit of the earth that needs to be planted and sowed and watered and cared for, not the strange fruit eaten by the oppressed, which leads to pain and misery.

I walked back into the room and shut the door to the balcony.

This time I had no trouble falling asleep. I slept until Doug wandered into my room. He took two more Xanax from the bottle I had left on the night table. He went out, to sleep again.

Now, I was awake. I couldn't stop thinking about sex. To hell with women. To hell with sex. To hell with Dylan. One more time it was all about Dylan.

The one time I went to AA, some old biddy kept saying 'Ya gotta pay the bar bill.' I knew she was right. Even the cute young girls all the guys buy drinks for, pay. Everyone does. Count on it.

I walked over to my backpack and took two pills. I thought I paid for everything when I got out of the hospital. Cancer was my admittance into the real world.

That old drunk got it right. We have to pay the bar bill. It always comes. This isn't about cause and effect, or crime and punishment, or some categorical imperative. It's all about getting something and giving something else up. If you were lucky you got what you paid for. I suspected that seldom happened.

The merry-go-round always stops. We all have fair warning but who listens? Who listens? Not I. If you did, you'd be paranoid and live on a psych ward and be stuffed with medicine to get rid of fear. The world conspires against realists, now, and forever.

I thought of Siegel. I wished Alex wouldn't be cruel to him. I liked to see Alex hurt Siegel, even though I became disgusted with myself for feeling that way.

Isn't that morality, feeling guilty for what you'd done? No I supposed not. Being moral meant not doing things you'd feel guilty about. I was no thinker. I was a guy coming down from too many pills, too many people, too many unpaid bar bills.

The thing about taking drugs is that your sense of time gets all screwed up, also that your sense of reality disappears. I wondered about the prophet preaching. I didn't even know if he was real. The sun had still not come up when I slipped into a heavy, dreamless sleep.

The morning came too soon, as mornings always do when it takes too long to fall asleep. I felt remarkably well after my mini-overdose. I'd decided to take Adderal so I'd have more energy.

Doug was still sleeping as Siegel pounded on my door. I opened the door and signaled that Doug was sleeping. I was about to say I wasn't coming either, but somehow I found myself getting dressed. I took a handful of steroids. They always made me feel better—what could they do? Make me even more impotent?

Siegel was pacing nervously as I exited my bedroom. I saw something feminine about him. It was his eyes. They were large and dark with long black eyelashes, but delicate, too delicate for a man of his size and power.

You'd say they were wasted on a man; a woman with those eyes would be a beauty, an absolute beauty. They seemed as though they would soon fill with tears. His eyes bothered me. We all wear masks, but Siegel's face was the mask, obscuring a sensuous woman gazing from within.

Time was passing. I got the rest of my gear and the two of us went to the lobby.

Escobar stood quietly with his friend, the Über guide, a basket of food and a cooler with water at his feet. He looked at his watch and at the elevator. The doors opened. Dylan and Alex exited, unsmiling but punctual. Escobar handed us each a bottle of water and urged us to drink.

"You must stay hydrated," he told us.

We all complied, deferring to his expertise and our own experience. Water was necessary, lots of it. We walked outside the hotel and entered the guide's car. He drove us down a side road into a clearing not too far from the hotel, where he parked. We ate some of the breakfast Escobar had provided, a basic breakfast of bread, some cheese, and some fruit. And more water.

I heard the whop, whop, whop of a helicopter as one of its blades created a whirling tunnel of air, which the next blade slapped. I shivered, remembering the huge turbulent vortex accompanied by a high pitch when I was in Iraq as helicopters came swooping in, a sound that meant death was reaching out for me. I heard that the Navy Seals had modified the helicopter it used to get Bin Laden, so that it didn't make that warning sound.

The helicopter landed. We scrambled in and grabbed seats. The helicopter took off before the doors were completely closed. Our adventure was beginning.

I saw Dylan's good breasts, her strong thighs, her caressing hands, and pleasant smile obscuring the memories of instant fatalities.

The guide didn't acknowledge any of us. He gave us the lecture about how things went bad fast, killing our innocent excitement. It may have been overkill, but it added to the adventure. We exited without a sound, and strapped on our skis. The guide gave a cursory glance and seemed convinced we were ready—or at least ready enough.

We looked around and saw long expanses of powder, steep hills, chill, and frost. The sun was coming up, a weak sun. The moon was still in the sky, the deceptive moon telling us that all was well. The snow was in shadows, ready to be awakened into brilliance, but sleeping before the start of day.

This is the crazy deep powder of a mountain peak. We got ready to ski down vertical ridges and boulder-filled areas that required our total concentration and all our skill, in defiance of gravity and physics.

The powder was untouched. We were silent. Even Alex remained subdued, in awe of nature in all its glory. Escobar waited, as did his friend. Alex jumped off one huge cliff and another. At times he flat-landed and fell over and tumbled down the slope, head over heels, but righted himself for another long run on undisturbed powder. I had forgotten how good he was, how much time he'd spent perfecting his skills.

Dylan followed. She was strong and graceful and fearless as she too skied down a vertical wall of snow. I skied and maneuvered the slopes well, moving toward the trees, avoiding the largest ledges and longest jumps. Escobar and the guide started out together but soon separated.

We had ample space. We skied, we jumped, and we soared into the air and landed and fell and right ourselves, each alone in this glorious world of speed and silence and beauty. Wherever you looked, you saw snow and mountains and mountains beyond the mountains. The boulders came on us rapidly but we jumped—they with ease and me with enough athleticism to keep safe.

The sun rose, illuminating the landscape with a beautiful golden glow, contrasting with the shadows of the trees, the ominous shapes of the boulders, and the pure snow. The snow gleamed white and clean, reminding me of linens in luxury hotels, of the pure shroud covering Dublin in its symbolic death and of the starched lacy dress of a little girl's first communion, before the disillusionment that must follow.

We skied until we couldn't ski any more. Our lungs burned. We were done, but we still had miles to go. Our mouths were full of the taste of fresh snow and sky. The brush embroidered the boulders with gray shot through with silver and enticed us to try to jump, as though we would fall upon soft pillows.

The sun rose in the sky, brightening the snow until it became a floodlight, causing our eyes to throb, impairing our vision. The clear white of the clouds merged with the terrain, interrupted by silvery trees and bushes, with their patina of some ancient cloth.

I felt the noiseless rush of speed and catching big air, gravity reminding me of its inexorable pull. Slowing down involuntarily I was exhausted, frightened. I did not want to soar like an eagle, nor zoom down slopes that rejected my essence.

I stopped and looked down. It wasn't far. I knew that I was safe, but I couldn't move. I stood frozen, having trouble breathing.

Dylan had crossed the terrain and came up behind me. She took in the situation in a moment, paused, saw I was okay, and flew past me down the slope. She jumped over a ledge and caromed out of sight.

I stood for another minute. I was cold but I couldn't move. With enormous effort, I pushed off, and starting skiing again. Powder hissed from my boots, but now I couldn't stop. All I saw was snow, above me, below me, snow and the sun and mountains. I told myself to enjoy this powder, this run, because I would never venture on skis again. I promised myself that as I labored over the ledges and boulders, with enough skill to get myself down.

A large conifer, a six-foot-ten power forward, was in my way. I realized that I would not win in any face off. I stopped, deferring to the immovable tree and slumped back into the snow, listening to the sound of silence. I heard the whoosh of the skis of my friends as they moved below me. The sounds faded.

All I could hear now was my own heavy breathing. I gathered my last drop of energy, got up, and skied down, suddenly feeling euphoric. I reached the bottom. It was wonderful.

I planned to meet Doug and get on a plane. That would be that. No explanations. No good-byes. No closure. They knew why I was leaving, better than I did myself.

I prayed to the God I didn't believe in that I would have the strength to leave this drunken life; that my friend Doug would stop drinking; that life would be tolerable. I wondered what that would cost me.

The price you paid for being sober was not drinking. The price I paid for a bearable life was giving up Dylan, ironic because I never had her.

Doug was in the lobby when I got back. He had his bags packed, us checked out, and a taxi ready to pick us up. Siegel had gone up to his room and Alex and Dylan were out looking for a drink.

I didn't know what happened in Aspen after that. I thought it could be anything, just not anything good. It would have been one from Column A and one from Column B—drinking, drugging, indiscriminate sex, self-destructive behavior, and malicious mischief. Oh yes, and great skiing.

Dylan and Alex would meet up with Dodo—or not. Siegel would leave. And they would all drink a lot. Drinkers are like that: predictable, sociable, and lonely.

Chapter 20

I took a quick shower and got dressed. Packing took about three minutes. I met Doug and walked with him to the cab without saying a word. We didn't even stop to grab something to eat. That's how much we wanted to get away. Goodbye to Aspen, to skiing, and to our friends.

Checking in at the airport took minutes. They were calling our flight as we walked through the gate. It didn't take long for us to get on the plane and get settled.

"I don't know, Doug. Wherever you are, it seems you want to leave."

"Yeah," said Doug. "I get that. I personally only have two problems. Albeit two is a very small number in the general scheme of things, they cause me much trouble. The first is that everywhere I go I want to be somewhere else. The second is that every time I'm someplace I don't want to be, I drink."

Doug snuggled into his seat and closed his eyes. I put my cap over my eyes, and fell asleep for a long and satisfying nap. The Captain's voice woke me up. We'd be landing soon. I checked my email. My editor had left a long message. Since Doug was coming along, we rated a Villa that ESPN kept for visiting dignitaries. We'd be staying at the Polo Golf and Country Club instead of the Breakers as originally planned.

I considered this a mistake. ESPN was letting me write the piece as well as take pictures. Now I would be in constant touch with the horses and groomsmen and exercise boys, as well as the polo players and owners. The less I knew the better. I'd noticed that readers preferred it as well. They liked to keep their uninformed opinions pristine.

Mine not to reason why. I had planned to spin my tale of grace and strength to the old folks at the Breakers, but it was not to be. This was far more modern and authentic. It would have a much harder edge. I had always preferred beauty to truth.

Looking around the terminal, I saw an international crowd. As we walked toward the baggage area, we saw a well-built, tall Hispanic man holding a placard in his hands that said Gosling. We gave him a friendly wave. He saw us and smiled.

Doug pointed to two bags on the carousel. The man easily took them, as well as one of mine. I'd borrowed a black bag from Escobar from the vast array of luggage abandoned at the hotel. All the bags left on the carousal were black. Most people tied a ribbon or strapped their bags to differentiate them. My bag had no such distinguishing mark. Not having a distinctive feature is a distinction. I waited. Doug waited. The tall Hispanic man waited.

People gradually removed the bags rotating around on the carousel, until only one bag was left—black, with no ribbon and no strap. Had to be mine. I smiled. The Hispanic man nodded and picked up my bag.

He carried the bags easily and escorted us to a waiting limo parked under a no-parking sign. After opening the door and helping us inside, he handed me a large manila envelope from ESPN. As we drove, I opened the envelope and found a note explaining the change of plan and the availability of a full-time cameraman for Doug. The staff had prepared lists of all the competitions, the players, the owners, and more.

Our man drove out of the airport. It seemed minutes until we were at the 1100-acre complex, which was the luxurious Golf and Tennis Club of Wellington, Florida. After a few minutes more, we were at our Villa, a large, semi-detached home in one of the prime areas of the property. I figured this place would sell between four and five million bucks.

We were living the highlife.

The driver had a key for the front door. He walked us inside and showed us where everything was. We thanked him, and Doug gave him a fifty-dollar tip, which the man pocketed with a smile.

He asked, "Is there anything else you need?" He handed us each a card with his name, phone number, and email, then grinned, and left.

Two golf courses, manmade lakes, tennis courts, eight polo fields, and a pair of croquet lawns were available for the members of this vaunted place. Wine tastings, holiday buffets, cultural outings and more were was offered when golf and tennis palled.

The restaurants were world class and the wine cellars superb. Perhaps F. Scott had it right after all.

The main attraction in Palm Beach this week was polo. Polo ponies got better treatment than college athletes, in terms of food and physical care, keeping in mind that the ponies were more expensive to begin with.

It was grand watching sixteen magnificent thoroughbreds maneuver over three hundred yards, with good-looking, athletic men guiding their every move. Polo players were athletes who did on horses what most men couldn't do on foot.

I was glad I hadn't been here two years ago. The romance was lost when twenty-one of Lechuza's beautiful horses died within a few hours of a big match from hemorrhaging in their lungs. It was a painful death. Dying in the interest of more stamina seemed gruesome to me.

Turns out it was miscalculation of the supplement mixture that did all the damage. Officials scrutinized the entire affair from beginning to end and found no evidence of foul play.

Now, two years later, the Lechuza team from Caracas was in the running for first place—again. Polo ponies aren't irreplaceable athletes. Poor dumb beasts.

Someone made a mistake and twenty-one thoroughbreds, trained and capable, had died. However, other thoroughbreds replaced them.

I'll bet they had more stamina.

I heard Doug wandering from one bedroom into another. He found five, a nice choice. He came into the living room, fingering his laptop and scrambling for his newspapers.

"Say, Doug, are you going to write anything for ESPN?"

"Nah. You want to use the photographer?"

"Sure, let him earn some money. I'd never take a pay check away from anyone."

I called my editor's assistant, told him that I wanted to take pictures inside the stable, and asked him to arrange it for seven-thirty in the morning.

"Could you set up a time to play with the tennis pro today?" Doug asked.

I called and learned that the head pro was "very busy." I agreed that one of his assistants would be fine. They arranged for a steam and massages at the spa after the lesson.

The atmosphere at the resort was electric, a mix of owners, players, and beautiful women, so many beautiful women. They were all thin and well-built, with beautiful faces and beautiful hair. You couldn't always tell how old they were, but the young were more stunning and more arrogant.

All the women wore big jewelry—bold diamonds, rubies, and sapphires—on the tennis courts, in the swimming pools, everywhere. Security staff, dressed in khaki pants and polo shirts, tried to be obtrusively unobtrusive.

After tennis, we went to a plush spa, with luxurious white leather furniture, glass and chrome tables and chairs, and softly colored wallpaper. The floors were glistening wood covered by yards and yards of oriental rugs, in subdued colors. It was light, airy and very quiet, as lovely women employees smiled pleasantly and spoke softly.

We poured lemonade from silver pitchers. I made a note to find out what a membership cost. Ice, loads of lemons, and precious little cookies, enhanced our spa experience.

The massage rooms were painted in soft shades of grey. My masseuse was a strong-looking, mildly attractive female, who gave me a few different oils to smell and asked me what type of massage I wanted.

I left it to her and tried not to be embarrassed by the scars from Iraq and from my surgery. She didn't mention anything, discreetly pummeling my body. I fell asleep and awoke only when she thanked me for allowing her to massage me.

Feeling refreshed and comfortable, we left the spa. Many golf carts were parked outside, with little banners flying from the top. We recognized ours, because it didn't have a banner. We slipped into the golf cart, electric of course, with no annoying noise, and drove back to the Villa.

Young folks were driving around aimlessly in the golf carts, drinking, laughing, and accomplishing nothing: the stupidity of second or third generation wealth.

Doug went to his room and worked on his new book. I went out on the terrace to read. A few minutes later I heard the door shut. He had left. I went back to work and didn't notice the time pass.

I studied the Lechuza team and planned the photographs of the stable and feed, the supplements and the trainers. I made a list of possible people to see. I liked the Argentian Captain of the Venezuelan Team, which figured to win the whole thing, new ponies and all. I made a note to ask if his ponies had survived.

I dozed off for awhile. When I woke up, I heard Doug come in. Doug was laughing out loud, as happy as I'd ever seen him.

"I just had a moment," he gasped, guffawing hard. "I went to walk on the beach and watch people. Someone saw me walking and asked if I wanted to borrow his scooter. I accepted his generosity.

"As I was riding, I passed an outdoor café and saw an obese woman in a belly shirt, which revealed a corpulent midsection. Her skinny, bespectacled husband sat with a cup of coffee. Eggs benedict, a double order of bacon, a bran muffin, and a chocolate malted were spread out in front of her."

"A lot to see as you passed by," I commented.

"I hadn't figured out the gears. I was riding slowly," Doug said. "The layers of fat around her stomach undulated in a perverse way into her shorts. I wondered how they made love.

"I couldn't picture it. It seemed impossible. It would be funny to give an 8th grade physics class the problem to solve. Maybe with a series of pulleys and levers, the act could be completed, but not without the risk of grave injury.

"How did the woman choose her outfit of the day? Did she get up and think I'm going to put on clothes that will nauseate all passers-by? She was hideous and in some way wonderful, with the temerity it took to be seen in public."

He was laughing even harder. "I don't know why. I couldn't help myself. I pulled the throttle and screamed 'Save some for everybody else!'"

"I drove away as fast as I possibly could and here I am."

"Listen, I have to go to the stables. Do you want to come?"

"No," he said, chortling to himself. "I think I'll stay here."

I got into our golf cart. I was beginning to hate riding in it, but I got in and drove over to the stables.

Chapter 21

Palm Beach erupted in a paroxysm of activity. The Polo Golf and Country Club expanded, energy extended in every way. Nothing and nobody was relaxed or serene. The place was jumping. Everybody was getting ready for the big matches. All of the matches, even the early ones, were well-attended.

The people were well-dressed in a Palm Beach way. Lily Pulitzer predominated, but some of the women tried for a dressier, more elegant look.

The resort was filled. Many guests in the Villas. The guests were assimilated into the restaurants and little picturesque wagons covered in tropical flowers, with discreet signs mentioning the goods for sale and no prices included. That old "if you have to ask" appealed to snobbery thing.

Breakfast wagons dotted the areas. The bar wagons had begun selling their wares, and the wares were extensive.

My cell phone rang with a few notes from Elvis Presley's *The Devil in Disguise,* the music I had picked for Dylan's ring tone.

"Hi," said Dylan in her husky voice. "Come have breakfast with us."

"Where are you?"

"Dodo was coming to Palm Beach, so we decided to hitch a ride. We're at the restaurant near the golf course."

"Let me see what Doug wants to do," I told her.

I went back to the Villa. He was up and having coffee.

"Do you want to meet Dylan *et al*? They're at the restaurant near the golf course."

"No," said Doug, "but why not? Which golf course?"

I talked to Dylan. We made some arrangements. She hadn't bothered to tell us which of the several restaurants near the golf courses she meant.

Soon enough Doug and I and our trusty golf cart made our way to the right restaurant. A buffet with every kind of breakfast food imaginable, omelet stations, a Champagne fountain, whatever, was laid out on at least four long tables spread about the room. No one had to wait for more than ten seconds to fill their plate.

Dylan and Alex were seated at a table for four outside the restaurant. We eased into our chairs and smiled at them.

"You're looking well," Dylan said.

"As are you," Doug answered.

A waiter came up quickly, leisurely dining sacrificed to the crush of polo madness. He took our drink orders and asked if we wanted coffee, which he poured into waiting cups.

Fireworks were bursting in the heavy air—American flags, parachutes, Saturn missiles, and sparklers, difficult to see in the sun. A mariachi band serenaded the breakfast eaters. I saw a few small trucks with other bands as well. The area was alive with music, noise, and laughter.

Some bagpipers marched down the path, piping away. It was a six-ring circus. As we ate our breakfast, people rushed in for picnic baskets. A large number of staff in various kinds of uniforms stood ready to obey our every whim.

"That's the best thing about being a drinker. Food isn't important," Alex drawled.

"Where's Dodo?" Doug asked.

"He had to see to his polo ponies. We promised we'd meet him tonight at the parties. I don't want to miss the parties," Dylan said.

"I'm sick of parties," Alex said. "I liked Paris better. We sat at cafes, and drank, and enjoyed ourselves. This whole country is tiresome. There's always something going on, and it's never worth the trouble to see what it is."

Dylan shrugged.

Alex ignored a group of Morris dancers as they cavorted about. A man dressed in motley, playing a pipe, romped around, followed by a large number of children and some young people in khakis and emerald green shirts.

"Summer camp for the children to keep them from annoying their parents. Americans do have some strange ideas," Alex said, and he smiled.

"What's funny?" Doug asked.

"I'm feeling good. Know how it is? You have a great buzz, but the room isn't spinning and you don't feel sick? All you have to do is go slow and you can go on forever. That's how I feel."

"Ah," Doug sighed.

"Yeah, but I have to keep drinking. I don't want to lose the feeling, and somehow I always get drunk," I said.

Doug sighed again.

Photographers were all over the place. Maybe some of them did work for magazines. They were taking pictures of the women and their families.

People were talking in loud voices. The music and the sound of firecrackers added to the excitement and the confusion.

The noise stopped as though a secret signal had been given. The spectators responded. The ponies were getting ready. It was quiet, except for the shrill laughter of a few women who had too much to drink. We were in a magic forest where nothing had consequences. You had a free pass for whatever you did or at least that's how you felt.

I drank the free champagne, which wasn't bad. I quickly stopped, thinking of the headache I would get. I didn't do well on sparkling wines.

Alex drank a bit. Dylan drank and popped pills. Doug told jokes and was jovial and drank maybe four cups of coffee. Nobody ate much.

Oh look," Dylan said. "There's Mary Jane Murphy."

"Goody," said Alex. "Yay." He was not smiling.

"Oh come on, Alex Bank. She didn't want to represent you because you write literary books. I don't see why you took it so personally," Dylan said.

Doug piped up, "What agency?"

"*Aaron Priest*," Alex muttered.

"They're good," Doug said.

Mary Jane walked toward the table, but did an abrupt ninety degree turn when she saw Alex. The woman with her stopped, staring at Dylan, who was just that beautiful. Mary tried to usher her away.

The woman was there for a conference of children's book writers, as evidenced by her name tag, which had a blue ribbon that said "author." She wore a light red and blue Chanel silk scarf draped over her shoulders. Her hair was dark blonde, with lighter highlights, and her makeup was discreet.

I knew the look. She was a well-dressed, well-groomed woman from the Midwest, trying to look cosmopolitan. She was trying too hard.

"Mary Jane, introduce us to your writer. I'll bet she's a big success," Alex said, with an earnest look on his face.

The woman seemed slightly embarrassed by the praise. Miraculously, she was holding Bernie Siegel's book. We all looked at each other, and laughed.

"What do you think of Siegel's book?" Doug asked.

"I loved his first book. He's a wonderful writer. I just bought his new one. I can't wait to read it," the woman said.

"Oh, you read?" Alex asked. "Do your books sell?"

"They do okay. My books are very popular, but only with a small audience."

"That can't be, not if Mary Jane represents you." He smiled charmingly. "Do sit down, ladies. This is a literary table. I'm sure you'll feel quite at home."

Mary Jane said, "I don't think so."

The writer recognized Doug and sat down. We all smiled at her, sort of like welcoming the latest cancer patient coming for chemotherapy.

Mary Jane tried to get the woman to leave but saw she wouldn't be able to. She gave a wave, departing with a look on her face that would have been perturbed if she didn't have so much Botox.

Dylan smiled and introduced everyone. The woman told us her name and said she was so glad to meet us. "My writing group will really be impressed."

Alex looked her up and down. "So do you sell many books?"

"I've done five books. They do pretty well."

"Oh," said Alex. "Did you think you'd sit at our table and we'd say, 'she's a writer. She has a beautiful scarf. She's a sophisticate.' Did you get an MFA?"

"Alex," Dylan said. "Come on."

"No, I want to get to know this lady better. I've always wanted to know what inspires someone to write children's books. Were you molested as a child? I think not. Even a perverted uncle could do better."

Doug looked into his glass as he finished two quick shots of whiskey. "There are good children's books. Think *Alice in Wonderland*," he said.

"So what's the name of your latest masterpiece?" Alex asked.

"*Will You Be My Father*?" the woman said. "It's about a child whose parents got divorced."

"Might be good for toilet paper. Why don't you take your knockoff Hermes scarf and your Iowa education, and sit at another table. Maybe somebody else won't know."

"Freud said hostility is generally a sign of sexual frustration," the woman said, trying valiantly to stand up for herself.

"Your next book could be *Dime Store Psychology for Five Year Olds*."

"Why are you attacking me?"

"You're an insult to all of us. Do you consider yourself a writer? If you write children's books, that's not really writing."

"That's your opinion. I consider children's books literature."

"Literature, literature. What do children's books have to do with literature?"

She is trembling. "I don't understand."

"I could explain it to you but I can't understand it for you," Alex said.

"What did I do to you?" she asked.

"You're here, with Doug Gosling, the greatest living American writer. You should have taken that name tag off and thrown it away."

I watched his hands, fists clenching, ready to attack.

"Your husband is laughing at you right now, lying in bed with a slightly younger version of you who's not even attractive. Probably a friend of yours. I can smell you—it's the smell of failure."

She was struggling to get up from the table. I saw her feet in neat brown oxfords, peeping out of an ankle-length skirt. She had tied her shoes with two neat, even bows. That made me very sad.

Nobody deserved to be attacked like that. She seemed so hopeful when she sat down, so excited to meet a famous writer, so innocent.

"Nothing to say for yourself? Sad comment for a writer. Of course I would expect that level of discourse from someone whose main character walks around saying 'I'm red, you're blue,' and asks everyone, 'Will you be my father?'"

"I'm sure the protagonist is adorable, a little baby panda who goes to the zoo and asks the zoo keeper, 'Would you be my father?' and he says, 'No, I killed your mother and you're next.'"

The woman stuttered, tears in her round eyes, makeup a little smeared. She tried to speak.

Alex interrupted her and said, "Wait, wait, everybody listen. What fantastic insight can you offer the world, Mademoiselle Simone de Beauvoir?"

I had to give her credit. She battled on. She said "I'm sure your life is solitary, poor, nasty, brutish and short."

"Ah, Thomas Hobbes. What would he say if he met you? Let's see—probably that you're a load that should have been swallowed, not worth a shilling. My God, woman, you are too stupid to insult."

None of us said a word.

"Why don't you get up and leave?" Alex asked.

She was silent.

"You came here with such hope and saw a great writer, a famous photographer, and a great beauty, and thought you could sit here."

I looked at her, steeling myself to say something, to stop the slaughter.

I saw her sturdy shoes on her little feet with the perfect bows, the scarf draped just so. She came into the bar with hope, a little hope, nothing great. She just wanted to be a writer among writers.

"That's enough," I said. "Please ignore this man. His behavior is inexcusable—and he can't get a book published no matter how hard he tries. "

"Oh shut up," said Alex.

"What can we expect from a man who holds the coats of his girlfriend's lovers?"

Alex jumped up.

I stood, walked past him, my shoulder hitting him firmly in the chest, as I helped her up, sheltering her from Alex. Her scarf was askew, her face streaked with melted cosmetics.

I held her arm as she limped away.

She walked out of the restaurant, despair etched in her face.

Doug followed me. We walked a while with no one speaking. We came upon a young, beautiful girl of about sixteen. She had a perfect oval face. People would think such perfection accompanied a lack of intelligence. I doubted the girl was stupid.

She stopped us and asked for directions. This floored me. She was where she wanted to go.

We continued on. I took some pills to avoid having to deal with Dylan on an interpersonal level. The problem with drugs is that when you're not doing them, life becomes unbearable and slow. You have this terrible habit of repeating yourself.

We got to the Pavillion and watched the rich and famous. Prince William and his bride were there. She was skinny, but sexy. The women wore their expensive dresses. The men, in their arrogance and power, were eating breakfast and drinking wine.

Alex came up behind me with Dylan and bumped me gently, as though nothing had happened.

"You know that moron Siegel is here. He's in the back somewhere. We have to get rid of him. He brings out the worst in me. Not much of a talent."

Dylan laughed. "Darling, you're a love. You don't need help to be impossible. I'll get rid of Siegel the next time I see him. He's a bore, but you know you are very malicious, very catty.

"If I wasn't, we'd have nothing to talk about," Alex said.

The horses were coming out on the pitch. God, they were beautiful. The riders were beautiful too.

A waiter was walking around with a tray of flutes of champagne. I took a glass. Doug took a glass. We clinked glasses and sipped our wine.

We watched the polo and everyone watched Dylan. She was more beautiful than the other women, taller and thinner; better, with a natural look. No airbrushed, plastic surgery for her. I think she was a modern-day Grace Kelly.

The morning stretched out into the afternoon, and one by one people left. We decided to keep going. What a shock to step into the Café Bliss, near the tennis courts, and find the whole gang, plus some owners and assorted hangers-on, sitting in a large booth.

I was glad Siegel wasn't there. Alex was uncontrollable around him. I drank my Stoli while everyone else had sangría. It struck me that people were saying interesting things but no one listened to what anyone else said.

Alex said, "You're mysterious, Dylan. That's your appeal."

Dylan said, "Deep down, I'm very superficial." She laughed her big laugh, and we all laughed as well.

Somehow, we were telling Doug stories. He good-naturedly listened and sometimes contradicted, sometimes added even more embarrassing details.

"Right. I should write a memoir of the ridiculous. It would be funny. I've never written a funny book. I'd love to, but you have to be willing to laugh at yourself. I'll do it now, in a bar, where nobody remembers what anybody says, but not in a book. I can be objective about anything, except myself."

I laughed. "So much for us quitting drinking."

Alex said, "I'm glad you haven't quit. I don't trust anyone who doesn't drink."

"I can't drink and write. It's the thing that keeps me from being a wet brain. You know, I feel life is a mechanical oppression, and what else other than alcohol is a mechanical relief?" Doug said

"I'd like to go back to the condo, Doug. Want to drive the golf cart?"

"Let's hit a few first," Doug said, wanting to get in a little tennis.

I agreed and we ended up playing with two of the female pros for about an hour. Doug picked the older woman as a partner, which surprised me. When we began hitting, I understood why. My partner and I tried mightily to win, but in the end, we failed. That's the thing about winners: they win. Everybody else just goes about their business.

It was very hot. We kept stopping to drink ice-cold water. Doug's partner kept sucking on orange peels. She would wipe her hands carefully, and then wham the ball across the net.

We had a little audience watching us as the sun beat down on our heads. We kept the ball in motion. At the end of our session, the crowd broke into polite applause.

I looked at Doug. Doug looked at me. We grinned at each other like two Barbary apes.

"Anyone for steam bath?" I asked.

"I'm up for that, whatever it is," my partner said, as the one who liked oranges melted away.

"Steam bath is a game from my youth," Doug said. "After we work up a sweat, say at tennis, we jump in a car, turn the heat up as high as it goes, close all the windows, and head to the nearest lake, ocean, or pool, and jump in. It's marvelous. Never caught on, though."

We walked to the parking lot where Maserati's and Ferraris shone in the hot sun. Porsches gleamed. One fat cab driver, slouching beside a dilapidated cab, saw us and smiled. I went up to him and asked if he knew of a private beach where we could jump into the ocean.

He smiled a sly smile and told me his friend owned a beachfront restaurant that didn't open until eight-thirty. I gave him some money I had crumpled in my pants. He smiled widely, exposing very white teeth, and told us to get in.

I asked him to turn up the heat and close the windows. We all got into the cab. A slight odor of fish emanated from the torn and creased leather seats. We three crowded into the back and began to sweat.

"Can we please open a window," she asked.

"*No se puede*," the cab driver said.

The drive was about ten or fifteen minutes but seemed like an hour, made bearable when the driver passed around an open bottle of some cheap red wine. It was lukewarm and a little sour, but as we drank, our spirits rose. The second bottle went down easier, as second bottles do as smoothly as fourteen-year-old scotch.

Soon enough, we were at the beach. The woman and I took off our shoes and socks. Doug threw off all his clothes and ran into the ocean. We followed his lead. We cavorted in the ice-cold ocean, throwing ourselves about and diving under the waves. After about four minutes, we danced out of the water.

The cab driver had managed to scare up a few dingy looking towels and even dry clothing. The woman, unfortunately, had to put on her sweaty tennis shirt, but did so gracefully.

"This is marvelous, just wonderful," she said.

"Grand, isn't it?" Doug asked.

I hoped there would be more wine on the way back. That would make it a perfect day. The cab driver found a few cold beers and turned the air conditioning on. That did make it a wonderful day.

We got home ready for a nap. As we walked into the Villa, the phone started ringing. My ESPN editor called to congratulate me for the preliminary article on polo, the one I wrote before I arrived, when I knew absolutely nothing. He wanted more.

I asked if he'd like something about basketball or a ninety-one-year-old marathoner.

"No. I'd prefer you to stick to polo. What did you think of the photographer we sent you? He's available and does great work.

"I haven't seen him yet, but I know him. He's a good guy, a real pro. I have a feeling he's seen it all."

"Yeah, Iraq, Afghanistan, Kabul. The guy's been around."

"How about Miami at night?" I laughed. "If you don't think it'd be too dangerous."

"Stick to polo, Pete. Keep up the good work. See you back in the Big Apple."

I'd never met a real New Yorker who called it the Big Apple. For them it was The City.

"See you," I said. "And thanks."

That gave me more time with the gang. Part of me hoped Doug would stay as well. He was a great guy to have around, one of the few who could hold his liquor and not get ugly, but he was already making noises about leaving. He didn't like Dylan or Alex.

I called Dylan. She answered.

"Dodo's friend is throwing a caviar and vodka tasting party. It's called for ten in the Amaryllis Room. Get there by 11:30," Dylan said.

"Sure," I said.

"Splendid," she replied. "See you."

My heart leapt to think I would see her that evening.

I took a long nap. I showered and shaved. I called out to Doug. He didn't answer. Life was better with Doug around.

Sad that life was not better with Dylan, but I found it bearable when I had the possibility of seeing her.

Rain began to fall. Soon it was pouring. I sat on the covered patio at the back of the house, staring at the golf course in front of me. The rain turned the paths muddy and the sand traps into shallow lakes. The last of the golfers were heading back to the clubhouse, one jumping out of the cart and hitting the ball intermittently.

These were shadow figures because the sun was hidden behind clouds. The rain came down harder. I smelled the ocean, or imagined I smelled the ocean, an overwhelming saltiness coming at me. I felt the shadows closing in.

There had to be a big sea and big waves breaking over the surf. The angry wind carried spray from the ocean miles away. That's what I smelled. I could swear it.

I saw the paths of the golf course. One bar cart was struggling to come in. The driver threw out large bottles of wine to lighten the load of the cart and continued driving. The wind pushed the cart about, a child's toy. It shook and twisted, but kept going.

The cart made its way to the shack where the golf carts were kept. Someone jumped out of the darkness and helped bring the cart inside. Both the driver and this person must have been soaked. I knew they got no bonus for their intrepidity. They were more replaceable than polo ponies. They cost far less and were not as well trained.

I saw the spectral figure of a man rush out and scurry down the path, retrieving all the wine bottles. He might return them to management but maybe not. I doubted he would.

I poured myself some Ketel One. I added as much ice as the glass would hold, then sat and watched TV for awhile. I had reached the stage in my life where I didn't care. I could sit here. I could play tennis. I could write the novel I had in my head, the one that kept rattling around. I could shoot myself. That would stop the pain.

I could smile and make a phone call. There'd be someone to marry me, some girl who'd convince herself that sex didn't matter, and it wouldn't until she got used to being married.

Not a good place to go.

I started counting my blessings. That didn't take long.

What does it take to be happy? What's a deal breaker? Sadly, you seldom find out until the deal is broken.

Maybe it was time for the world to end. Maybe the earth was too tired to spawn anything but pain. No love, no tolerance, nothing but a vicious jungle of existence, down deep in the heart of men. Maybe Conrad really had it right— the horror! The horror!

Hard to say.

I looked outside. The rain was coming down hard, the wind uprooting trees.

I started laughing. That was a good thing. I picked up the phone and called the tennis court bar. They were open.

"Thank you," I said, and hung up.

I headed toward the bar. My phone rang. It was the theme music from *Jaws*, which I had recently chosen for Dr. Turk.

"Hey, Petey. All is good, but you need to come back in. I want to take another look at you."

"I'm in Florida. I won't be back to New York for a couple of weeks. Do you want me to come back now?"

"No rush. Call me when you get home."

I instantly felt at ease, knowing there was no rush.

Then Turk said, "Don't forget to call when you come back."

Why did he have to say that, I wondered.

"Should I be worrying, Doc?" I asked him.

"There's nothing to worry about. Petey, you're fine. I'm just being careful."

I wasn't worried, but I sure needed a drink. The first thing I saw when I entered the bar was a huge crowd. They'd lit a fire in the fireplace. It was beautiful. A big stone fireplace and a big fire blazing away. Someone was playing a piano, ragtime, fast and furious.

The waiters were refilling pitchers of sangría, bringing daiquiris and piña coladas and wine and martinis and straight liquor. The rain was a good thing for the waiters and the restaurant, a very good thing indeed.

A table of people, polo players and their ladies, team owners, Dodo and others, and Alex and Dylan in the middle of them, were laughing. Is it a gaggle of polo players?

Dylan sat on one side, talking to a good-looking young polo player. She was speaking softly and quietly. When I came to the table, she looked up at me, annoyed.

I nodded and took a step as to move on.

"Petey," Alex said. "Where's your sidekick?"

"Taking it easy for a few days," I said.

"Yeah, all that writing is strenuous."

Alex was slurring his words. "His friend is Doug Gosling, America's greatest living novelist," he said.

Everyone continued with their conversations, except Dylan.

Somehow, the spell was broken. The polo player stood quickly. He wasn't tall, but had broad shoulders and a narrow waist. A young girl, no more than seventeen, got up as well, a bright smile of relief on her face.

Dylan looked at me and then at the girl, who ran over to the polo player and grabbed his hand. The polo player started to say something to Dylan.

Dylan had turned away. "Your loss," she said, and turned to speak to one of the owners.

He bent over her, lighting her cigarette.

I knew as no one else did who would be in Dylan's bed that night, or some night soon. These things have an inevitability about them that no one, not even Dylan, could change. The kid would do whatever it took, as would Dylan. This was not fate but character.

Wasn't it Shakespeare who said 'love was madness, and lovers should be locked away and treated harshly?' Perhaps that was what Dylan needed, or deserved.

Once again, a feeling of *malaise* passed over me, and once again, I shrugged it off.

Alex started drinking in earnest: whiskey. A practiced drinker, he wouldn't mess with fruit, schnapps, or whatever else they threw in the sangría. That only made you sick. No need for that.

And out of nowhere, Siegel appeared. It wasn't his night.

He came upon the group and apologized. "Sorry, guys. I didn't know you'd be here. I'm meeting my publisher and his wife. I'll mosey along until they have a table ready for us."

Poor sap. I believed him. The fates were conspiring against him, as they had for a long time.

Siegel tried not to look at Dylan, but he had to look.

I watched as the adoring man who would do anything for Dylan disappeared. For her, the dance was over. The music had stopped. This was the forest primeval. I saw it in the flash of their eyes, in the veiled contempt with which they viewed one another. Deny it at your own peril.

It was an old dance, known at some atavistic level to all the players. Those who danced best knew the tune and were prepared for the danger. They came, as did Dylan, heavily armed.

As Siegel stood there fighting with himself, a young looking, well-dressed man with white hair and white teeth approached him.

"There's a table for us in the back," he said.

Siegel took his arm, and the two walked off. The white-haired guy caught sight of Dylan and stared at her as though she were a life preserver and he was drowning.

The waiter shoved another chair in at the head of the table and put some Stoli in front of the chair. I sat there and started drinking. Some of the people spoke Spanish, a language I knew well. The women were catty, the men admiring. They all smiled as though they were praising us to the skies.

Alex introduced me. One of the men said hello.

"That was a wonderful article you wrote about us. It was very fair."

"I like to think it was true," I said.

"Fairness and truth don't always go together. You are not a polo aficionado," he said.

"No. For me, *afición* is for bull fighting, but that's a dying sport."

"Yes, it's difficult to find young boys willing to die for passion," the man said.

"Maybe bull fighting is different because our sympathy is with the bulls. They're easy targets," one of the Spanish beauties said.

The man I'd been talking to laughed. "Oh yes, easy targets."

Dodo nodded at the beauty and said, "It takes great courage to face the bull. Anyone who has been in a bull ring knows that."

He was courtly, which made him seem pleasant.

"And, good sir," said the man, "have you faced a bull?"

"No, I don't have that much courage," said Dodo.

He did confess, not to cowardice but to a certain lack of courage, and in doing he so seemed brave.

The man raised his glass to Dodo. "Ah, yes, you are a friend of a good friend of mine, Jonathan D'Angelo. He has spoken of you with great praise. If you see him, please tell him Victor Vargas says hello.

He turned to his companion. "Come, my dear," he said. "It is time for us to go."

He got up, as did the Spanish beauty who talked of bravery. Sometimes what passes for bravery is sheer ignorance. This woman possessed much of the latter. As has been often said, perhaps in other words, it is better not to speak because you won't confirm an opinion of yourself as foolish. One wonders why the need to speak foolishness is so compelling.

The couple left as Dodo rose from his seat, murmuring his farewell.

"Señor Vargas confuses movement with action. That is fine. His Spanish beauty is capable of issuing enraging statements. Best that he left," Dodo said.

"Is that his wife?" I asked.

"Never underestimate a man with a beautiful wife," Alex said.

"I only think that's true if it's his first wife," I said.

"Pete," said Dodo, putting his hand on mine. "I do not know how you do it, but you set me at ease and allow me to feel comfortable. You are a good man.

"This is getting much too serious," I said. "Anybody hear any good jokes?"

Alex said, "I have a funny story that happened to me the day before I returned to the States. When I came home, a credit card bill was sitting on my table. I stared at it. It didn't return the stare. I didn't open it. It could have cared less."

Nobody laughed.

Alex raised his glass, as did we all.

"Here's a toast to people who make toasts."

The table fractured into separate conversations. After a time I looked at Dodo. No one was listening to us.

"How do you stand these idiots?" I asked.

"I don't," he said. "I do admire your friend Doug, though. You know—everyone thinks they're capable of writing a

THE URGENCY OF NOW

novel. They might be able to, but writing it well is another matter. Doug does that. I've never thought much of talent or ability, but execution matters a great deal to me.

"Mr. Gosling is a serious man in a world of silly people. I think he drinks as much as he does because it's difficult to face who you are when you're that good."

I pulled out my cell phone to see the time, and was astonished to see how long we'd been sitting there. Dylan and Alex melted away. I didn't sparkle enough for them. I guess I needed Doug as a ticket into the higher realms of being.

No problem for me. I took my bag of soggy clothes and got into my trusty golf cart, heading back to the Villa. I wondered why Dodo deigned to talk to me. I thought it was because I was too inconsequential to worry about.

I fumbled for the key to the Villa and found it in my pocket. I unlocked the door and went inside. I sat in the dark for some time, wishing things were other than they were. Dylan didn't mind how things were because she operated in an alternative universe. Drugs did that for you, at least for a time.

I felt empty and weak. I had done too many drugs for the second time in a matter of weeks. I passed out and when I came to, I was sitting in my chair covered with a blanket. I wanted to get my pills but couldn't get up. My whole existence was throbbing pain. I tried the meditation exercises. I tried visualizations and affirmations but never got beyond the first word.

I heard a loud knocking at my door and hoped it was a vicious serial killer. I wanted to shout, "Come in, you're welcome here!" I was crying. Dylan burst into the room and stopped, looking at me with such compassion.

"You've got to cut down, sweetie. These drugs are killing you," she said, with no judgment in her voice. "Where's your stash?"

I pointed weakly to the little mini-bar.

She walked over quickly, opened the door, and saw my vast array of pills. She picked one up and looked at the others.

"Two green—one red—on the first shelf." It took me a minute—sixty seconds, to get that out.

I was sweating and crying and shaking and still filled with pain. This wasn't supposed to be happening. I was in remission. The chemo had worked.

Dylan came over and put the pills in my mouth and then added a little water as well.

"Swallow," she said.

I tried but the water dribbled out with some vomit and blood. I blacked out.

When I came to, Dylan was cradling my face in her breasts. Hopefully I had swallowed the pills.

She gave me a few more. This time I kept them down.

"You are so good, Petey. I love you so much. I'll take care of you. Don't worry," she crooned. "I'll always be here for you."

The pain had settled down into a dull roar—bad but tolerable.

The thing about Dylan is she believes what she says, at least for the moment. She would give it a shot. She's good at the grand gesture. A lot of people are like that. It's the day-to-day stuff that's hard. You have to love somebody more than yourself.

Sometimes that doesn't happen until you have children. When my parents saw me moaning in my hospital bed, either one of them would have jumped in and taken my pain.

As much as Dylan meant what she said, it would always be someone else she'd want in the bed. Maybe if she had a child it would be different, although I doubted it. Right now I didn't care. She cleaned me up and held me, and that was pretty good.

I was dozing off and felt Dylan's tears on my face. Maybe I was wrong.

I slept for hours and woke up as Dylan entered the room holding a tray of food. "Here's something for you. I know you didn't eat anything. I have enough food for Doug as well."

"This is so nice of you. Thank you."

"What are friends for?" she asked. "You have to stop taking so many pills."

"I know," I said. "I know."

She busied herself with the food—clams on a bed of ice, white wine, and bread. She put the clams on a plate with a bowl of sauce, and poured the wine into a glass. She handed me toast with jelly and a cup of tea.

"I'll take the clams," I told her.

"Eat your toast," Dylan said.

I declined and grabbed her plate.

I dipped one of the clams in the sauce and ate it. It was fresh and tasted of the ocean. It must have been shipped a few hours ago. The wine was cold and good, expensive.

I thought about Dylan and how nice it was that she came by. She fell asleep on the couch.

I lost the feeling of being worn down and unable to act. The world came alive with possibility. Maybe things would get better, a whole lot better.

Dylan kissed my forehead lightly, her lips barely touching my face. She shut the door quietly as she left.

Chapter 22

I'd had one of the best night's sleep I'd had in a long time. I decided to write a blog.

Blog about Love

> *"There must have been moments even that afternoon when Daisy tumbled short of his dreams—not through her own fault, but because of the colossal vitality of his illusion. It had gone beyond her, beyond everything."*
> —F. Scott Fitzgerald, *The Great Gatsby*

> *I don't have the objectivity to have any insights. I know a lot of my love is my creation and my need, but it doesn't make me love her less. I love all of her, her eyes, her smile, her laughter. I love her golden hair. Her beauty kills me. She controls my very being; all else fades into nothingness.*
> *Millions of people travel miles to view a small picture of a woman smiling. When I see her, I see the Mona Lisa. I see the bone chilling perfection of beauty.*

*Why can't she love me? I could give
her happiness from my love alone. It is
incomprehensible anyone else can feel the way I
feel about her. How it hurts me when she tells me
others have loved her the same way. This is not
possible.*

*I think one day she'll understand. I hope it's not
too late.*

I got dressed and went to the stables. It was busy. I saw ancillary staff who took care of the horses, as well as security and people from the feed companies, making sure no one made mistakes with the feed or supplements. There'd been many lawsuits. Nobody wanted any more.

I guess they call that locking the barn door after the horses have left the building.

People from the hotel complex stood at regular intervals all through the barns, scrutinizing passes. They turned away several people whose credentials did not pass muster. This was the first day of the matches. Security would intensify as timed passed.

Sam, the cameraman, came up to me as we met one of the vet techs, who'd been there two years before, who tried to comfort the horses when they died. She'd been too new to be allowed to do anything else, leaving her without guilt or shame. She still had to live with the raw pain of horses dying with their heads in her lap.

Everyone walked about with some purpose or other. The horses ate their food, watching the activity about them.

Sam, a guy I'd always liked, took a lot of pictures. He made sure he got photos of everything but looked to me for cues. I deferred to his expertise. They say the advantage of getting older is that you get wiser. I don't know about that, but I did get more careful.

When I was young, every day mattered, but life was going by and I wasn't moving at all. I was opting out more and more. This was alarming, but I couldn't seem to find anything to do about it.

The horses snuffled and made quiet sounds. The techs did their jobs quietly. Even security was circumspect. I didn't know if the barn was like this before.

I asked the young tech. She wasn't gorgeous but had a nice smile. I had the feeling that she would be a lot lower maintenance than the beauties who would be coming by later. She calmed the horses as she patted their heads and checked their legs. It would be nice to be with someone who contributed to serenity instead of chaos.

The riders began straggling in. Their leading scorer came in looking like hell. He'd had a hard night and was still half in the bag. Some of the other riders teased him genially, but the Captain of the team, an Argentian, scowled as he pulled him into the corner near me.

He spoke in Spanish, but Sam gave a running commentary, not knowing I understood every word.

"What are you doing? Are you able to ride? Are you able to play?" the Captain asked. "You're not fooling anyone. You're using again."

"Sure, sure. I'll take a shower and shave. That's what I need."

"After the fourteen-year-old girl and rehab, you don't need this," the Captain said. "Vargas has had enough. Not that I blame him."

The man staggered a little as he moved off.

Polo was a rough game. These guys made it look easy but many men, many horses, and a lot of money at stake made it very dangerous. You needed all your wits and all your reflexes. Alcohol was no friend of either.

The captain moved on without looking at us.

"Thanks, man," I said to Sam.

"No *problema*," he replied, with a laugh. "Will you use this?"

"Nah. He's got enough problems."

Sam looked at me with approval in his eyes.

"Don't think I'm worthy. I'm not ambitious, which allows me the luxury of scruples. Life isn't hard to manage when you've nothing to lose, and believe me, I've got nothing to lose.

"I think it was Abraham Lincoln who said 'When I do good, I feel good; when I do bad, I feel bad, and that's my morality,'" Sam said.

"That only works if you're moral," I said.

Sam looked at me. "Morals are allowing someone to make a paycheck even when you don't need him. It's truly an honor to work with you. Your pictures are inspiring."

We continued, me taking notes using my recorder, Sam taking pictures. We got some great shots of the people, of the horses, of the food supplements.

I went to lunch. Sam had taken off to get his photos ready for me. We had more work to do.

People milled about, walking or riding in golf carts.

Professional dancers filled the open areas with pirouetting, swaying, skipping, prancing, and cavorting about. They wore bright costumes. The best dancers came from Brazil and were doing a hot samba.

The women were delicate, but with large breasts. They danced in 4/4 time, with a syncopated beat. They took back and forth steps, tilting and rocking their bodies, shaking every part of themselves in times to the music. It was sexual and idiosyncratic.

Somehow, Dylan was in the middle of the group, wearing all white, standing there swaying and shaking her body in time to the music. The dancers were dancing with her, moving their bodies rhythmically. Dylan smiled as though she didn't have a care in the world.

As the dancers moved on, she walked into the restaurant. Onlookers applauded. Many of the people had cell phones and were taking pictures of her. All of the beautiful women stood helplessly as she stole the scene. She was Dylan. Wherever she was, she took command.

She laughed to herself as she walked through the restaurant. Her confidence was supreme.

I followed her into the restaurant, feeling one hundred percent invisible. What chance did I have? What chance had I ever had? When it comes to true love, there were no happy endings. Sad, more than sad. In my own way I was as pitiful as Siegel, maybe even worse.

I gave my name and was led to a table. Dylan slid in next to me. Alex came in a few minutes later, followed by Siegel and his publisher. Dodo and Vargas walked up to us, paused, and sat across the way. They stood when Vargas' woman and two young, beautiful girls walked up to the table. The group sat and began talking.

Dylan looked at me with raised eyebrows. "I had thought better of him," she said. "How borrrrring."

My cell phone rang. It was Doug. He wanted to make sure where we were.

"Yeah, we're at the usual restaurant. It's crowded, but we have a table."

"Great. I'll be right there."

The restaurant was packed. Many people were sitting at the bar, eating, and drinking. They allowed smoking. The women smoked cigarettes. Some smoked cigars. Some of the men were smoking Cuban. The odors of expensive perfume, rich food, and Cuban cigars merged with the smoke and wafted on the air. It was the smell of money, the smell of privilege, the smell of ultimate power.

Vargas' woman got up. Dylan slid out of her seat and walked over to her. She whispered something in her ear. The woman said something to Vargas. She left and Vargas smiled.

An attractive older woman walked up to Vargas and said hello. He half bowed, but did not invite her to sit down.

"She must have been a beauty in her day," I said to Doug.

"Catherine, the patron saint of the older polo players, plays a little herself. The lady is from Argentina, from a poor family. She married a much older man, a finance minister when she was sixteen and pure. He was a very brutal man. His hardness hardened her. Catherine washed up in the United States. She became fabulously wealthy by building an international jewelry designer company from nothing," Vargas said.

"Wow." I said.

"I know her. I met her a few years ago," Doug said. "She can outdrink a Marine, has great skill riding a horse, and she's damned willing, which makes her damned good. She is self-centered, self-absorbed, and excellent company."

A waiter came over and asked if anyone wanted a drink. That took precedence over any conversation. We ordered our drinks. Doug had a hot tea. The rest of us had booze.

I went outside. It was raining. I was looking for Dylan but couldn't see her. When I went inside she was sitting at the table with our friends. Vargas' woman was gone.

By this time the table was several drinks ahead of me. I ordered a Jack and Coke. It went down smoothly. I noticed a small chip in the glass. I hoped it had broken years ago. I didn't want to swallow glass, but even more than that, I didn't want to send my drink back.

Doug was laughing and telling jokes—and still not drinking.

"Never trust a man with an ugly wife," he said. "For me the perfect woman is Helen Keller inside Scarlett Johansson's body."

Charming," I said.

"It's about as charming as asking a woman how many men she's slept with," Dylan said.

Doug recognized the polo player I hadn't written about and insisted he join us. The fellow tried to order a drink, and Vargas shook his head.

"Don't be so stuffy," Dylan said.

"He'll have a glass of champagne," she said to the waiter.

Dodo got up and walked to our table, overhearing the conversation.

"Leave him alone, Dylan. He's fighting his demons."

"It always amazes me how moral everyone is for everyone else. The fewer morals someone has, the more they want everyone else to behave well," Dylan said.

"My, my," said Dodo. "Malice does not become you, my dear. You should keep away, you know. Your ways are careless and dangerous. *Cuidado.*"

Dodo bowed as he kissed Dylan's hand. He turned and took the hand of one the young beauties and escorted her from the restaurant.

"Was that a threat?" Dylan asked.

Vargas shrugged. "He's right, you know. The kid deserves better."

"There is nothing better than me," Dylan said.

Alex ordered expensive brandy, and everyone other than Doug and I had some. They drank more.

Doug was pouring sangría into everyone's glasses while drinking hot tea from a delicate china cup.

A busboy came by and tried to clear the table. Alex picked up his drink and jostled the boys arm, causing some liquid to spill on Alex's trousers.

"Great, just great. Do you know that my pants cost more than you make in six months. *Hablo? No hablo?*"

"Leave him alone, Alex. It's enough," Dylan said.

"It just occurred to me. He's the only one in this room Dylan hasn't slept with."

He turned to the waiter. "*Desea esta belleza mujer?*"

"Alex, you've got to stop. It's enough. You're getting obnoxious. It's embarrassing." Dylan said. She was beautiful but looked tired.

"Who are you" Alex asked, "to decide how I should behave, and what I should say? I could just imagine being married to you. I'd have to sit in a corner and raise my hand if I wanted to say something. You know, Dylan, you're getting too big for your britches, to make a pun of it. I think you're forgetting what you came from."

"I think you're mistaking me for some of the women you hang out with," Dylan said in a mild voice.

Alex was ready for another target. He gave a horrific smile and turned to Siegel. "What are you doing here, Bernie? Do you belong with us? We're people who enjoy having fun. Why not say something? Defend yourself."

"Ah, the words of a true anti-Semite. When you're attacked, get angry at the Jew," Siegel said.

"How intellectual," said Alex. "An existential coward. You are a coward, you know. Do you think Dylan wants you here? What do you bring to the table, some hamantashen?"

"You know," said Siegel, "it's time for me to take off. This is who you're with, Dylan. I know it's not for the money. Do you feel you can control him? You're not superior to him, you know. You're not. You're worse. I'm sorry I intruded."

He got up and walked away.

"Hurrah! The odious minority group has left the building," Alex said. "I'm not anti-Semitic. It's him. I hate that guy." He started to cry.

Doug finished his cup of tea. I got up. Doug got up. Dylan sat there, staring straight ahead. She was sitting right under one of the lights. Her face was a mask, a death's head.

I walked outside, sickened by them all.

Humidity washed over my face. The downpour was over. I saw the treacherous moon, duplicitous and disloyal. The wind dried my face as it danced over the leaves and the trees. I heard a band playing across the way, but couldn't make out the tune.

Three short men, or perhaps boys, were taking advantage of the dark and the rain. They grabbed boxes of food and cases of wine and shoved them into a truck. The truck was white, like those of the Polo Club, but with no writing on the side.

A fourth figure jumped out of the truck and yelled at them, the sound muffled by the wind. One small shape returned to the crates, refusing to leave and was shoved aside by the fourth man. He fell to the ground as the three others jumped into the truck.

He got up hastily and followed them, greed dissipated by fear. I vaguely wondered if they would be able to get out of the gated area. I was half rooting for them. I'm no admirer of Robin Hood, but I sometimes wonder why seven-eighths of the world doesn't revolt and grab the riches of that small, condescending minority.

It's the phenomenon of sheep herded by a shepherd and one small dog, bred into the shepherd and bred into the sheep. These men, or boys, or women, were not escaping their fate, but merely digging a hole into which they would fall—sooner or later.

Still, I cheered them on—the small, rag tail band of marauders. I guess we all love underdogs, probably because we are them.

The people standing under big golf umbrellas seemed not to notice the brazen theft, or perhaps they, too, were underdogs, in their own minds. Perhaps so. Some got into their golf carts.

I was sick of golf carts. This place was a geriatric world, where people raced to get to their nursing home beds or their graves. I was sick of the glamorous people. I was sick of everything. The worst thing about cancer is the way it sickens your soul, coloring the world with the same disease as your body.

Doug, my savior, a voice of reason crying in the wilderness, drove up in a golf cart.

He said "Beep. Beep. Care to join me?"

I got in. The moon cast a silvery glow on the people standing there. The band packed up their instruments and stepped away.

Sam, my cameraman, was busy taking pictures of the crowd, the lake, the moon, and the pilfering.

He waved at me and I waved back.

Dylan came out and walked toward us.

"No fireworks tonight, gentlemen," she said.

"Oh, I saw fireworks," I told her. "They weren't very attractive."

"Come back inside," Dylan said, as though I hadn't spoken.

"This young lady wants a drink," Alex said.

"Yes, she does," Dylan agreed.

We came to a tacit agreement and went back inside as if the whole scene had never happened. All the emotion and malice and despair had disappeared. We were a group of friends out for a pleasant evening.

The restaurant was even more crowded. A small jazz band had set up in the back. They were good. A female singer had an amazing voice, no one was listening. The conversations grew louder and louder. The musicians were playing for each other and enjoying themselves.

"I'm going back to our place," I said. "I have a lot to do to get ready for tomorrow."

"I'm ready to pack it in," Doug said.

"I'm going to stay here," Dylan said.

"I'll stay," Bernie said.

"Then I'm going," Dylan said.

"No, I've had enough," Bernie said, and stormed out.

"Do you care who you hurt?" I asked her.

"Oh stop it. You all bore me. We're supposed to have a few laughs, some champagne, and go back to whatever we planned to do. Everyone understands that, or they should."

This was a funny conversation. She was nervous, twisting the ring on her finger, playing with her hair.

"Let's get out of here," she said.

"Sure."

"Do you have a bedroom for me at your place?"

"Yes, but I have to go back there and do some work."

"Pete, I need you."

"I think we both know that's not true. Sometimes you have to do what's right. It can't always be about you."

"Once upon a time, it was all about me."

"Maybe I'm getting scared in my old age. I've got my own worries."

Dylan looked at me and smiled her old sweet smile. Tears came into her eyes. "I'm sorry, Petey. I'm being selfish. Let's have one drink, and I'll go back to my hotel."

She took some pills from her purse and swallowed them without water.

"One drink. What's the harm?"

"Dylan, please."

"Don't you love me anymore?"

"That has nothing to do with it."

I was annoyed. She was a taker and a user and I loved her.

"Why is everything such a drama? Why are there always terrible consequences to what you do?" I asked her.

"Petey, I'm selfish. That's me. People get hurt. I haven't changed since the day you met me."

I looked at her, at the curve of her lip, the shine of her eye, the little tears that were appealing, and the slender body with its curves. She was beautiful.

She looked up, the tears in her eyes evaporating. "I need someone to love me. What can I do?"

For one brief second I wanted to tell her I had cancer and thought better of it.

We left the restaurant and walked together on the fragrant, flower bedecked paths, lit by a moon shining murkily in the sky. When she put her soft little hand in mine and pulled me back toward the restaurant, I didn't pull away.

"I suppose I should find Alex," she said.

"Maybe you should," I said.

I climbed into my golf cart and drove back to the Villa. The air was redolent with fallen rain and the heavy perfume from tropical flowers.

Men in uniforms were out and about, removing fallen branches and leaves and broken flowers from the paths and gardens. By the time the guests awoke, the grounds would be repaired, nature enhanced into perfection by human hands.

EATUP

TRY OUR SELECTION OF TASTY, HAND-SELECTED BOXED MEAL OPTIONS ONBOARD!

Now available on select flights.

JETBLUE AIRWAYS

NAME BLUMENFELD/ANNA   MRS

20NOV

FQTV B6 2012725450   NFUJEU   BOARDING TIME

FLIGHT 39

NEW YORK JFK
WEST PALM BEACH

GATE 02   SEAT 19E   700P

                                        OK TO BOARD

                                            SEQ147

BOARDING PASS

E   TIC
1 279 2 8   30 6

Chapter 23

I worked for about an hour. Sam had done a masterful job, making mine a lot easier. The piece ended up being good. I saved it in three different places and sent it off.

I remembered how difficult things used to be before digital photography and computers. I wanted to be a purist and claim I did better work when it was me and my camera. Everything wasn't better before.

Being young is better, but that can't last. If I cared, I'd be interested to see who would prevail, Dylan or Alex. I don't think I cared.

Alex always had money. He didn't have the benefit of poverty. Some of the owners had suffered great poverty and no matter how much money and status they attained, the merciless nature of their childhood, inexorable and overweening, would prevail. People raised in destitution were always prepared for adversity. Great joy might be beyond their grasp, but the vagaries of fortune would not ruin them. Siegel and Alex didn't have that protection, and neither did Dylan. Her beauty would only protect her so long.

I went to bed, making sure to take enough pills to let me sleep the rest of the night. I slept the sleep of the dead.

The phone rang a couple of times. I ignored it.

I realized I'd agreed to meet Sam at the stables at 7:00. I sprung out of bed and called him. It was after eight. He told me to go back to sleep, that he'd cover for me.

"Let's meet at the restaurant by the tennis court at 11:00," he said.

"I can't thank you enough, Sam. If there's ever anything I can do for you, just let me know."

"You know, there's another story here," Sam said. "Team Jaccara didn't come to the meet. Their owner got involved with a sixteen year old *au pair*. He could be arrested if he comes back to the States."

"I could see how that would be frowned upon," I said. "I'll take a pass."

We hung up. I took a long shower and shaved. I was foggy from the pills. I knew what to do about that. Pills are better than booze. A little of this, a little of that and you're as good as new.

I checked my voice mail, email and text messages. Nothing of much interest, except Siegel's many missives, looking for Dylan. God, what a pest he was.

I decided to walk to the restaurant, which was a mistake. The trip was a lot further than I'd thought. By the time I'd realized it, it was too late to go back.

Doug and Alex were sitting at a table by the bar, a big pitcher of orange juice between them. Their laughter made it clear something other than orange juice was in the orange juice.

A waiter came around with flutes of champagne. I shrugged him off.

A woman walked by and said, "It's been too long."

Doug greeted her warmly, but didn't introduce her. After a bit she walked off.

"I have this horrible habit. If I don't want to sleep with a woman, I can't remember her name," Doug explained.

"I've got to have some food," I said.

Sam walked in and sat at our table. "Good morning all," he said. He was smiling. I caught a faint tinge of stables. I think he'd changed his clothes, but horse was horse.

He gave me a large yellow envelope that I put under my seat.

"I can't thank you enough," I said.

"Dirty pictures?" Alex asked.

"No," Sam laughed. "Polo ponies and feed, vitamins and lots of security, as though they could change the past."

Doug said, "A common human error, which I practice often. I'm Doug Gosling, nice to meet you."

Since Sam had met Doug the day before, he looked a little puzzled, but stretched out his hand to shake Doug's. Sam and I went to the buffet and got massive breakfasts: Sam deserving of one because of his hard work, I because I hadn't eaten much since yesterday morning.

We filled our plates. A waiter also got omelets for us and brought them to the table. I gave him a twenty-dollar tip, which wasn't too well received, and stuffed another twenty in his jacket pocket. The waiter returned with champagne.

"It's not bad stuff," Alex said. "You should try it."

We imbibed, sitting peacefully, eating our food, sipping our champagne, and enjoying the good life.

The crowds had thinned. The polo players and owners and their entourages were gone, as were a lot of the spectators. They came for the polo. That's where they were—at the polo match, making things much more pleasant for us.

Things got uncomfortable when Siegel walked in.

"Where's Dylan?" he asked, in a subdued tone.

"Tell me," Siegel said, becoming more agitated.

"I stopped looking for her a long time ago. When she wants to be with you, she will be. Can't you get that through your thick skull?" I said.

"You're insulting, Petey. I don't know why. Where is she? I want to know now."

"I don't know. I don't know! Obviously not here. You know you're crazy," I told him.

"Where is she?" Siegel asked.

"Figure it out," Alex said.

Doug joined in, "I guess you don't know her better than I do after all. I was right. She found somebody better than you."

"Siegel, you're the fraud of the western world—and Doug, you're no better," Alex said.

Siegel looked at him. "At least I know I'm a fraud."

"No pretense about that—or about Doug. Doug is a lot of things, but he's not a fraud," I said.

"I wish I were a fraud," Doug said. "Then at least I could have a moment of happiness."

At that moment, Dylan entered the room.

Alex saw her. "Enter Ophelia," he said.

Dylan walked up to the table. She sat down without looking at Siegel. It's funny how women can do that. The guy was big and hard to miss. He was staring right at her. She sat as though he weren't there. The scene was set. It had to be played out. No one could stop it, least of all, me. The table grew ominously quiet.

The silence was interrupted by someone calling my name from across the room. I saw George, one of my favorite people, a really great guy. He was on the short side, maybe five eight, with long, heavy arms. He didn't look too impressive in his clothes. I smiled at him and waved him over, happy to see a friendly face.

I stood up and hugged him, feeling how powerful he was under his loose shirt and unstructured jacket. You wouldn't think he was a middleweight champ by looking at him. No one recognized him. They didn't know who MMA fighters were, let alone how tough they had to be.

"This is the gang. Everyone, George. George, everyone. He's the UFC Middleweight Champion of the world," I said. "How's the poetry going, buddy?"

George smiled. "My poetry has improved a lot. It's hit a new level, awful."

"A fighter who's a poet. Siegel is a writer who's a fighter. Perhaps you two should have a rhyming contest. Siegel, how does Ode to a Jew go?" Alex said with a sneer.

"Dylan, we need to talk," Siegel said, ignoring Alex.

Dylan looked at me, "Let's go. I need to get away from this crowd."

Siegel grabbed Dylan's arm. "You're not going anywhere. I need to know where you were. We need to resolve things."

Alex answered, "Oh, we've resolved things. You're a total boor. No one likes you. Dylan has destroyed another wasted soul. Petey is impotent. George is going to be the poet laureate of the United States, and I'm bored by this, and you."

Dylan shrugged off Siegel's arm and got up.

Siegel reached for her wrist, half-crying, half-yelling, "No, I have to talk to you. Please."

"Let go, you're hurting me," Dylan said.

"Let her go," Alex said, not standing up.

Siegel was stone cold sober. "I need two minutes with Dylan, to talk to her, to explain things," he said.

"Don't you ever give up, Bernie? It's over. Actually, it never began. Let go," Dylan said.

I saw Siegel's grip tightening around Dylan's slender wrist.

"It's enough," I told him. "Stop it."

"Who's going to make me? You, Petey? Who? There's not a man here. Which of Dylan's pathetic minions will come to rescue the damsel in distress?" Siegel said.

"You're pathetic," Alex said. His malice was overt, spreading a shadow over us all, like kerosene near a lit match.

Siegel ignored him. He grew more menacing and growled, "Any takers?"

"Why don't you let her go?" George said.

"Be careful, champ. Siegel was the International Jewish worldwide boxing champion of Princeton, New Jersey," Alex said.

"Shut up," Siegel replied.

"Let go of me," Dylan pleaded.

"No, not this time," Siegel said.

George got out of his chair, grabbed Siegel's arm and pulled it away from Dylan.

Siegel threw a punch at the champ, which George avoided. He instinctively countered with a left jab.

Bam. Siegel was on the floor, supine, face up on the ground, knocked out.

"I'm sorry," George said, "It was a reflex."

I said, "Let's get out of here. You don't need this."

"I didn't mean to hit him," George said. "I'm sorry."

The two of us walked away from the table before anyone saw what happened. Dylan disappeared.

Alex grabbed Doug. They got up, trying to avoid unpleasant publicity. Doug had had enough troubles in his life. This wasn't his fight, just another mess caused by careless people who had never faced serious consequences.

Alex was holding his drink. He turned and slowly poured the drink over Siegel's body, from the top of his head to his feet, as he lay supine on the floor under the table.

Two waiters came up and carried Siegel out of the room. If anyone noticed, no one said anything.

Sam sat at the table, finishing his food. I was surprised he was still eating.

"Hi, Champ," Sam said.

"Sam's taking pictures with me." I said.

Sam finished his meal. He joined us as we exited the restaurant.

"Oh sure, you did that spread about best pound for pound fighters for *Sports Illustrated*. Thanks for including me," George said.

"You're one cool customer. I'm impressed you finished your meal," I said.

"I learned that in Afghanistan. Never leave your food unless you're going to be bombed." Sam laughed.

We were walking as we talked. I had seen all the messiness. What we had here was a mess. We walked past an outdoor café. A few people were sitting there. They didn't look good.

Sam gave George a card. George walked down the path toward the parking lot. Alex had wandered off. Doug was gone.

Sam walked in a different direction. I'm not sure where. I had to get to the polo fields. Notwithstanding Sam, it was time for me to earn my keep.

Chapter 24

I got to the Polo field. I heard screams, sirens coming from every side. I quickened my pace. I heard more loud noises.

There had been a huge accident. One of the polo players had taken a terrible fall. An ambulance was taking him away as I got there. He was wearing the colors of Lechuza. I couldn't see the number. The EMT's were working over him triple time as they put him into the ambulance, oxygen over his face.

I saw them relax as the doors were closing. They took the oxygen off his face. He was dead. They were trying to keep it quiet for the moment. No harm in that. The show must go on.

Vargas was standing near the ambulance talking to one of his players. They were both angry.

"Inexcusable," Vargas said. "The Audi player should be banned for life."

Things got quiet. People were saying that the guy was dead, but no one knew for sure. Lechuza won the match and the championship. There was no celebration. A thirty-five-year-old man, who was playing because another player had sprained his ankle, was dead. He had a wife and children.

I went back to the Villa. I put the TV on and poured myself a drink.

Sam had taken a phenomenal picture of the Audi player, half throwing his adversary off his horse. The horses were beautiful and graceful. The Audi player looked bored. The Lechuza player was out of his saddle. His foot was caught in the stirrup, his head dragging on the ground.

I did a synopsis of the story with the final two pictures: the Lechuza team holding the Championship Cup above their heads, and the ambulance driving off the field.

I went to the beach and walked along the shore. The sky was dark and foreboding. The air was alive with the promise of a storm. The sea was angry now, and ready to strike. I saw a beach chair facing the water and sat in it. The chair was sandy. I could feel the grit getting into my clothes, my hair, and my teeth.

I wanted to run into the ocean and swim until I could swim no more, swim until the water took me, and I breathed no more. My future was as empty as my soul. I had tried, and I had failed.

I sat there in the dirty deck chair—damp, tattered and abandoned.

I got out of the rickety chair and walked back to the condo.

Doug came in. I could smell whiskey on his breath.

"Petey, you won't believe this one. I'm walking home when a Bentley almost hits me. I give 'em the finger. The car swerves twice and goes through the window of a Dunkin Donuts. That's taking the drive-through concept to a whole new level. Broken glass, bodies, and donuts are everywhere."

I looked at him without saying anything.

"People are lying down, either badly hurt or ready to sue. I picked up a jelly donut that rolled close to my feet. I had an urge to take a bite but I resisted. You'll never believe who was in the car—Alex and Dylan. Alex, that sick bastard, jumps out and is screaming at everyone. Dylan looks sullen. Alex screams 'You crazy bitch'."

Doug continued, "He sees me and yells. Calls me a crazy bitch too. The cops take them both in the back of a squad car. The crowd is getting a little restless. A detective gives me his card, asks me for an autograph. I sign Norman Mailer. Don't know why. He doesn't say anything. I figured you'd want to call. I'll say this for you, Petey. Your friends are never dull."

Doug and I sat in front of the TV set, which we hadn't bothered to turn on. I called the detective and Dylan. Neither one of them answered.

I heard a quiet knock on the door. I opened it. Dylan was standing there. Doug excused himself politely. Dylan wrapped her arms around me and held me tight.

She pulled me over to the couch and we sat very close to each other.

"It was awful. I told Alex we were done. He started to cry. He seemed at peace. I thought he knew it was time. He asked me to take a ride with him," Dylan said. "I had one of these moments when you know you should say no, but you say yes. He was a little drunk, but he's been a little drunk since we first met. He said he had to 'scare up a car.' He begged me to wait for him. So I waited."

Her voice was hoarse as she finished her tale.

"He took Vargas' car. He almost hit Vargas as he drove off. I could hear Vargas screaming 'Stop. Stop.' I told Alex to stop, but he paid no attention to me. He drove for about half a mile. He had this terrible look on his face. He started to say horrible things about me and you. He said I was in love with you. I told him that who I loved was no concern of his."

She looked up at me and said, "He then turned the car violently. It almost flipped. He drove right into a donut store. He was a lunatic. He got out screaming. The police showed up. Alex kept yelling, 'She killed them all. First you killed them and then you killed me.'

"Miraculously, I don't think anyone was hurt that badly. The police officer asked Alex whether I was driving, thinking that's what he meant when he said she killed them all. He didn't realize Alex was talking about Cohen, you, and everyone else. Alex told them I was driving and that they had to arrest me?"

I held her close to me, trying to comfort her.

"A crowd was starting to gather, seeing a bunch of workers lying in the street around a Bentley. It was getting very unsettling. Finally, Vargas showed up and told the cops it was

Alex. Through the whole ugly mess I had one thought: I had to see you. I'm shaking, Petey. It was so horrible."

"It's okay," I told her. "Everything will be okay."

"I'm alone and unwanted," she said.

"Dylan, you're a survivor. You'll be fine."

"I don't want to be a survivor. That means I failed," she said.

"Who would have thought Alex would be so crazy," I said. "I'm so sorry it turned out this way."

"I really don't expect these things to end well," Dylan said calmly.

I put my head on Dylan's breast. I heard her heart beat, thump, thump, thump. My first thought was *what a wonderful thing; she has a heart after all.* I was lost in it. The pulse in my ear was one with her heartbeat. For one brief moment, I thought we were meant to be.

We lay there for a long while without saying anything. I began to feel light headed.

"You'd better call EMS," I said.

"Why?" she asked.

I'm dying," I said, as I passed out.

When I opened my eyes, I was in a hospital bed, with tubes and IV's and lots of beeping noises. I felt as if I'd swallowed a roll of nickels. Dylan was beside me, asleep in a chair.

She opened her eyes. They were bloodshot and beautiful.

"You're going to be okay," she said. "The doctor said it was probably nothing. He just needs to run some tests. He said no matter what, it's nothing serious. You'll be fine, honey. You'll be out of here by this weekend."

I wanted to believe her. I tried to speak, but the tubes stopped me.

She handed me a piece of paper and a pen. I wrote, 'You're the only woman I've ever loved.'

She read it and smiled.

"I love you too. I don't need anyone else."

She started to cry.

I was happy. My eyes closed.

About the Author

The Urgency of Now, Dennis Shields' second book, establishes him as a seminal thinker and a serious humorist. He is an international businessman, storied *raconteur*, sportsman, and man about town. Some say he has the mind of an Einstein, the wit of Oscar Wilde, and the good looks of a movie star. Others don't. He is a citizen of the world.

CPSIA information can be obtained at www.ICGtesting.com
Printed in the USA
BVOW011334111112

305168BV00002B/5/P

9 781935 254744